A Darling in your Fifties

ASHMI

First published in 2016 by

BecomeShakespeare.com

Wordit Content Design & Editing Services Pvt Ltd
Newbridge Business Centre, C38/39,
Parinee Crescenzo Building, G Block,
Bandra Kurla Complex, Bandra East,
Mumbai 400 051, India
T: +91 8080226699

ISBN 978-93-52016-39-6

Disclaimer

Law, police, and UN procedures have been kept as realistic as possible but these may differ in actual situations. This novel is a work of fiction.

Dedication

I take pleasure in dedicating my debut novel *A Darling in Your Fifties* to the great versatile actor, Bobby Deol, whose films have amused and prompted me to muse over love-hate relationship. The feeling of hatred for someone who had been special in one's life is more intense in many instances, for nothing else hurts more than being disappointed by the person you thought would never hurt you. This concept is well conceptualized in Bobby's film 'Humraaz' and it is this film that plays a significant role in the life of Neema, the protagonist of the novel.

ACKNOWLEDGMENT

First and foremost, I would like to thank God for giving me the patience and inspiration to write this novel, which had been my dream for the past many years.

I am eternally grateful to my parents, who instilled in me the value of education, especially my father who encouraged me to believe that one day my dream of being a writer could come true, if I chased it with single mindedness.

To my daughter, Smera for constantly encouraging and supporting me in achieving my dream.

I thank my friend and editor, Susan Helene Gottfried for reading my book with great patience and telling me several times not to head hop. I loved her comment when she said, 'Oh, I love this story.' Thank you, Susan.

My thanks to the entertainment industry as well that provides us with amusement and enjoyment. As the entertainment industry grows, we grow and evolve with it. Thanks to our Bollywood films that many times have a huge positive impact on our perceptions and cultural trends. Some films even have the effect of purgation on our morbid emotions.

I'm grateful to the entire team of the self-publishing company, WordIt.

PROLOGUE

On that stormy, stygian night, deep in the heart of some mysterious woods, she lassoed him to the monstrous branches of a banyan tree with determined grit and resilience and began to lash him ruthlessly in the fierce downpour unleashed by lightning and thunder, so fierce and violent as if the wrath of Kali was suddenly thrown up to bring justice to womanhood.

He hung, like an animal prepped for slaughter, his arms stretched on either side over his drooping head. A thin, snaky slick of hair dangled from his balding head onto his puffy cheek. Done in and famished, he raised his cat-like, bleary, green eyeballs and threw her a feline stare in the midnight darkness while she brimmed with wrath and grabbed her pocket knife and rived his chest with unresolved vengeance for all the emotional pain he had inflicted on her ever since their marriage. Licking his trickling blood from his hairy navel, like a frenzied maenad, her sporadic, joyful scream cut through the moist, chill air and her freaky, sardonic laughter trailed in the arboreal wind and was swallowed by the dark chasms, while his sonorous screams drowned and died in the thunderous claps that threatened another violent downpour.

Her anger like the volcano of Mount Etna being vented on that moonless night, she gazed up at the cleaving sky with a long sigh of relief.

Standing tall and firm in her black leather outfit, she smiled and watched his breath rise and fall in dry and tortured paroxysms from under his drooping head. She spit and squashed the heap of wet leaves under her high heeled boots, as she stepped close to him, unflinchingly, with an elated smile. His vicious stare wouldn't deter her anymore. She cocked her ears and thought she heard her father's words echo from the distant void in solitary hollowness: 'Girl, the banyan tree is the tree of life, in front of which married women worship to seek long life for their husbands.'

She turned her head towards the distant void with a sardonic smile before she turned back to the buckled man and wondered whether his limp body was still throbbing with life.

#

Neema woke up with a start, her head throbbing. The horrible nightmare had resurfaced again, throwing up her buried thoughts and feelings.

Arjun had married her with no intention of being a husband to her and had drained the nectar of her youthful life, rendering her a mere breathing piece of bagasse. Neema flapped her tearful eyes drowsily in the dark. An eerie loneliness crept over her. Eight and a half years of coitus banishment! A hermit's retreat in bed! A life deprived of hugs and amour. Cast aside, ignored, leaving her a mere zombie. Tears gathered in her eyes and made sleep impossible, although her heavy lids begged to be shut in peace, drowsy and sluggish with fatigue and somnolence.

On other nights, the empty space of her queen sized bed would be occupied by her daughter, Goldie, but these past three days it had been populated by pillows, as little Goldie was holidaying with her grandparents. A three-day closure of her school following a school day celebration had given the kid the chance to enjoy.

Neema sat on her bed to thank the great Lord Almighty for his wonderful gift—a gift that filled her life with a purpose and offered her a will to live, a gift which she cherished every moment of her life and that was Goldie! The kid was everything to her. Without her baby, she wondered what she would have done with her aloneness.

A gust of chill wind blew through the half-open window from the post-rain, cold night outside. The pouring monsoon shower had dubiously ceded. Neema rubbed the goose bumps on her arms and slipped back into the warm sheets.

Where was he, her husband, Arjun? Where could he have gone? There were times when he had disappeared thus, but not for over three days. A fourth day, too, had passed and there was no news about him.

She rolled on her belly and tried to shut down her turbulent thoughts, but they rioted inside her head. She had begged him earnestly to point out her errors, if there were any that might have displeased him, but he had always evaded responding. He had always chosen to turn away without ever making an effort to hide the little, sly, victorious smile on his big, slimy lips.

Those disturbing thoughts paced restlessly inside her head. Sleep was impossible. Her throbbing, pulsating cells needed to be silenced. Silenced by assuring, loving hugs.

She grabbed the pillow and held it tightly to her bosom. She closed her eyes and lifted it to her face and noiselessly began to rub her mouth on it. Her vulva shrieked desperately for a devouring carnal embrace. She longed for a man's assuring caress. Clutching the pillow, she dug into it with her nails, smacked it with kisses, and ultimately gave a copulatory moan. Her ruffled emotions began to allay. She softly cried into her pillow before she dozed off in the loving arms of Hypnos, never suspecting once that Arjun's neglect of her was intentional and preplanned and that he was having the ride of his life with a card up his sleeve.

CHAPTER ONE

Neema's mother, Kanthi, couldn't fall asleep either.

After a sumptuous dinner, while her second daughter, Mili, who was three years younger to Neema, took to her studies, Kanthi strolled into her bedroom and tried to grab some sleep in the hope of shutting off the disturbing thoughts she was assailed with.

She lay on her back looking up at the dark ceiling with a clenched teeth and evoked the chain of events that had taken place.

Eight years ago, her evil intention of zapping Neema's happiness had prompted her to make that eventful trip to Hassan, a small neighbouring town, a four-hour journey by bus from Bangalore, on a cold November morning, while her husband was still fast asleep in bed.

Jayamma had sent a missive to her through a neighbour of hers, a missive that had made Kanthi sit upright on the sofa with a glint in her eyes.

Jayamma had been a cook in Kanthi's parents' house in Mysore many years ago and was now living in Hassan as a widow with a grown-up son. She had spoken of a prospective bridegroom for Neema in her missive and had said that he, Arjun was a practicing lawyer in Bangalore and the only son of a respectable family who Jayamma knew for the past many years. However, she had said that the young man was not inclined to marry yet, for reasons best known only to him. But if Kanthi could turn him around, the alliance would be one of the best and would further strengthen Jayamma's friendship with the said neighbour, who was held in high esteem in the little town.

This missive had brought Kanthi the much-needed sigh of relief from the tormenting anguish that had developed in her mind, out of her craving need to jail Neema to a permanent ill fate.

Arjun? The name sounded somehow familiar. Sitting on the couch, sipping her noon coffee, she had tried to recall the piece of news that she had happened to read a few months ago in a vernacular newspaper about Arjun, one from Hassan who was arrested for having contrived a false document and released on bail hours later. The small black and white picture of him was not very clear, but not totally imperceptible.

She could not remember of any action having been taken against Arjun, the offender. The papers did not carry any news about it later.

He would be visiting his parents during the weekend, Jayamma had informed Kanthi. If it was the same guy, Kanthi had concluded, she could use him to her own advantage.

In the morbid darkness of her room in the wee hours of that hiemal Friday morning, Kanthi had hurriedly zipped her black canvas kit⊠ bag and told Mili, who sat on the bed drowsily with her back against the wall watching her mama, that she would be off to Hassan for a day or two and would explain to her everything after she returned. Warning the girl strictly not to spill the beans, she softly closed the main door behind her and hurriedly walked down the windy, silent street under an ash grey sky, her Mysore silk sari billowing in the chill wind of the November dawn.

She had boarded the red government bus to Hassan at quarter to eight, settled in the window seat, and lapsed into scheming… pondering a seminal plot that had come to occupy her mind.

It was almost half past twelve when the bus reached Hassan. Passengers jostled restlessly to get off. If the driver had not started that tiff with a farmer, who had placed his gunny bag of two huge jackfruits in the centre of the aisle, probably they would have arrived a few minutes earlier, Kanthi muttered disapprovingly as she got off. She walked a few paces and summoned a rickshaw.

As the vehicle zoomed past tidy, modest, silent houses on Temple Street, Kanthi couldn't resist an awkward simpering. *Arjun, lawyer from Hassan?* She became more or less convinced that he was probably the same guy who was in the newspaper.

*That too, one who was not much inclined towards marriage?
Who else could help her in shoving Neema to a corner, if it was*

not for this man? Only if she could clinch him as her son-in-law . . . She chewed the idea with pleasure, smiling to herself, her temples passively resonating.

The rickshaw suddenly halted in front of a bamboo gate that hung crazily on its rusted hinges, having slipped from its iron hasp. Kanthi paid the driver and pushed the gate, its creaking sound announcing her entry.

Jayamma quickly peeped through a corner of the square lattice window of her small kitchen, on which a calendar was stuck from the inside as a defense against the afternoon's blaring heat.

Though Kanthi's eyes wandered the entire façade of the little cottage, she failed to see Jayamma's face in the window, as the faded wooden sash presented only a square, tiny, dark hollow space and nothing else. Jayamma, stroking her neatly combed hair and cotton sari, hurriedly came out to welcome Kanthi with a huge grin, ushered her in with utmost warmth, and immediately unburdened her friend's shoulder from her kit bag and served her a glass of cold water. She battered her with questions about her health, family, children, the big town, and other household matters.

Kanthi, having settled happily on the single bed placed against the wall in the little breezy hall, exclaimed, 'We have lots to catch up with!' while Jayamma bustled about in excitement.

Years ago while in their adolescence, in Kanthi's parents' house in Mysore, Jayamma and Kanthi would spend post lunch time sitting on the cool granite step in the portico of the large house, playing snake and ladder or knitting sweaters while Kanthi's parents would be napping. Jayamma, being three years older, had come to treat Kanthi as her younger sister, and as such, even after her marriage at the age of eighteen, she had continued to work in their house, bound to their love and affection. Three years later, Kanthi too got married at about the same age. Even after Kanthi left her parents' house to move to Bangalore with her husband, Jayamma had continued to serve Kanthi's aging parents for many more years until Kanthi's father passed away one fine day after a morning cup of coffee around the age of seventy-four, two years after his wife's death.

Jayamma now busied herself in the kitchen while Kanthi changed and washed herself in the cement-floored bathroom to the far right corner of the wide backyard that was capacious with an enviable garden of fruits, herbs, and flowers.

The aroma of freshly filtered coffee wafted to the backyard and Kanthi strode in, feeling relaxed and happy to be served by Jayamma again. After an hour, Jayamma took her into the kitchen, suggesting that they have lunch together. She spread a pallet on the clean, cool, red oxide floor and set the hot dishes on the floor with a pair of steel tongs and placed large steel plates and glasses.

As Jayamma opened the lids of the dishes. Hmm … Kanthi inhaled deeply as she was served with delectable white rice, beans cooked in masala gravy and garnished with mustard, lemon and grated coconut, palatable tomato rasam, and spicy papaya curry garnished with aromatic curry leaves and cilantro. They did not stop conversing as they ate. In the course of their conversation, Jayamma assured that she would invite Arjun for breakfast the next morning so that Kanthi could meet him and have a talk.

Babu, who owned and drove an autorickshaw, returned in the night and was delighted to have a guest at home. He had met Kanthi only once many years ago, but said that he couldn't remember the encounter. He wasted no time in running the errand of inviting Arjun over for breakfast. Arjun, on the other hand had tasted Jayamma's tasty cuisine and gladly accepted the invitation.

At nine sharp in the morning, he cheerfully turned up in a pair of casual brown trousers and a T-shirt. Kanthi was introduced to him. Jayamma offered him water and cautiously hatched the topic of marriage. Kanthi observed his wide mouth twist in displeasure and when Jaymma turned towards Kanthi and told her with a simper, 'He is not much interested in marriage,' Kanthi immediately cut in, 'My daughter too has never been interested in marriage.'

Though Jayamma failed to understand why Kanthi was saying so, she let go of the sentence and chimed in, 'These youngsters must marry at the right age. Arjun's parents are already angry with him for continuously postponing marriage. Am I right, Arjun?' She directed her gaze towards Arjun.

Arjun scratched the back of his head with the tip of his right index finger, scrunching his face. Jayamma soon said that she would serve them breakfast and disappeared into the kitchen. She employed herself happily with serving them piping hot idlis with blobs of butter and coconut chutney and scurried between the hall and the kitchen while Kanthi slyly observed Arjun, as he ate religiously, intermittently asking him casual questions regarding his job and parents.

He was eating with his head bent down. His pate was more or less bald. A few long strands of haywire hair were oiled and discreetly combed in a thin spread across his pate from his left temple. Whenever Kanthi spoke, he arched his bushy eyebrows and briefly scratched his creased forehead with the back of his left thumb without lifting his face from the plate. It seemed to suggest that he toyed with thoughts which he kept to himself and if at all he smiled, it was a wily smile instantly summoned onto his thick, slimy lips.

'How is your practice going on?' enquired Jayamma when she came back with a tray of coffee. He threw a quick glance towards her with his marble-like green eyes. 'I'm doing well,' he said and coaxed her to eat her breakfast as well and not to be formal. After their cups and plates had been cleared, Jayamma cast an aphoristic glance at Kanthi and threw a hint to Arjun with a cheerful grin, 'My friend Kanthi has two beautiful daughters. Her first daughter has come of age and if you are interested . . .' She trailed off, creating a dramatically indefinite statement and looked at Kanthi, who was staring at the floor. 'Kanthi, you can speak. I'll go to the temple and will be back in half an hour or so. If you'll excuse me, Arjun . . .' She turned to Arjun and made it sound more like a question.

Arjun grinned and nodded and thanked her immensely for the delicious idlis and coffee and invited her to his home when she was at leisure. Kanthi felt a huge feeling of relief, as she had taken care not to disclose any of her secretive thoughts to Jayamma.

Arjun sat cross-legged and scratched his brow with the back of his thumb. 'Mrs. Kanthi, actually I wish to state...'

'I know you are not interested in marriage, Arjun,' Kanthi intervened gently. 'Neither has my daughter been. Your parents have shared this piece of information with Jayamma and when my friend informed me about it, as a matter of fact, I somehow felt, er, maybe here was the right match for my stubborn, headstrong daughter.' She gave him a dismal smile and looked into his eyes as if searching for an answer.

He threw up his head and gave a big laugh. She had said 'right match.' He heaved a deep sigh with parted lips and fixed her with a glint in his marble-like green eyes. He looked into her face gravely with puckered lips. Yet he was aloof, undoubtedly. A number of thoughts had invaded his mind.

Maybe he should just go ahead and get married. Here was someone who was telling him point-blank that the girl too was not interested in marriage. Here was someone who belonged to his own religion, to his own community, and that was what his parents needed. Moreover, Jayamma had already pronounced that Kanthi's daughters were beautiful and the mother had pronounced that her daughter was headstrong. It wouldn't be too difficult to break the marital bond after the tie-up. This marriage would certainly please his parents.

After a long, calculated silence he declared, 'I don't mind being your son-in-law.'

Kanthi couldn't believe her ears. She stood up with a grin. He was the same person who was in the newspaper. She could remember his face she had seen in the paper.......a guy who least thought that even a typical housewife like Kanthi, in her late fifties, immersed in her everyday chores, would have paid attention or bothered to take note of an inconsequential little piece of news that had appeared in some inner sheet of the newspaper featuring a tiny, scrambled black and white picture of him. *A blockhead swindler?* She couldn't suppress a lopsided smile.

It was a moment of victory for Kanthi. She didn't know then that Arjun's victory had transcended hers and that he was more jubilant than she was, as things had suddenly become easier for him at a time when he had begun walking a tightrope, which she was least aware of.

She hadn't been able to sleep all night. Being an early bird, no amount of restlessness would strap her to the bed. With the faint light of dawn seeping in through her bedroom window, Kanthi stirred and sat in her bed in a state of narcosis. Arjun had done his best to knock off the zestful spirit of the proud girl, had done his best to make Neema file for a divorce, but unfortunately, the girl had gone on with her life as if nothing had happened. She just seemed to be enjoying with her little daughter.

Kanthi heaved a deep sigh and plodded out to the bathroom.

CHAPTER TWO

Neema woke up, too, with the draught of chill wind fanning her from her slumber. She recalled with a faint smile the sexual satisfaction she had sought the night before with pillows in her arms.

The dull, faint morning light beginning to seep in and a lone bird, merrily, fluttering and chirping outside forced Neema to stir, lest she be late for work. She slumped on the edge of the bed and yawned disinterestedly, her bare feet sentient to the chill, glassy vitrified floor. Pulling herself up reluctantly, she strolled to the bathroom and lounged in the wide corner of the green marble bathtub with her toothbrush in hand and began to ponder her disastrous marital life. He was four days gone and had not returned home. Nor was there any phone call from him regarding his whereabouts. He had not even bothered to enquire about his little daughter, Goldie. Not that he had shown any fondness for his kid at any time or given her extra attention.

Forty minutes had gone by in the bathroom.

As she hurried to the kitchen through the commodious dining hall, a cast of golden light on the floor of the vestibule to her left caught her attention. With a mixture of scepticism and wariness, she paused and headed towards it. The light was from the hundred-watt bulb in the living room casting its yellow hue through the wide open doorway. The uncleared vittle on the coffee table caught Neema's attention. Remains of spicy, soggy peanuts and slices of blanched cucumber on a white corolla tray were lying bare, mobbed by flies. A bee hummed around the mouths of emptied liquor bottles.

He had come home! Stepping back to the dining hall, she shot a look up towards his room. Halfway up the white marble stairs to the right, on the middle landing, was Arjun's room; its thick, sturdy, single rosewood door was shut. It was always shut, making it hard to tell if he was at home or not. She let her gaze descend to the generator, beneath the climbing curve of the stairway. It was long dead as much as he was to her. She had gotten it repaired a few times, but then had given up when it had crashed again and again as much as he had. She had given up asking him about his whereabouts.

She retraced her steps back to the living room, picked up the tray and the bottles to be disposed, and eventually hurried through her organised routine that was habitual and quotidian.

Had he come home silently in the night? Where had he gone all these days? Had he brought home another person in the night?

She fought to shake away those disturbing thoughts with her morning chores but could not help faintly pondering over it as the thoughts lurked somewhere deep in her mind.

When she finally dressed and dashed to the garage and opened its shutter, panting, the fact that her car could be gotten out only after he had removed his Mercedes stared her in the face, to her dismay. She rushed up the porch steps gasping and her sari puddling over her toes.

'Remove your car, please,' she cried out, agitated, standing outside the threshold.

This was almost an everyday amercement for putting her car inside the garage. She knew he was in his room and had certainly heard her. The presence of his car was proof enough of his presence at home. Locked in his room, he might have even anticipated her agitated call. With a serene smile, he had continuously underplayed his stubborn refusal to make extra space for her car in the garage. It just meant removing much of the junk that he had brought from his parents' home. She had pleaded several times, but he had always turned a deaf ear. Now, she stood under the porch coughing, sweating, and waiting for him to show up. They had been married for over eight years now and she was well familiar with his disposition. He had always clammed up and been taciturn, while her own propensity to open up spontaneously had dropped by degrees, finally leaving her dysphoric. None of her entreaties or her queries in all those years had received a tangible response from this man who she hated now to even acknowledge as her husband.

She rushed back to the garage. She didn't have a second to spare! Standing by its open shutters, she screamed towards his bedroom window, which was right above the garage. She could see his shadow hover near the window behind the white net curtain covering the huge glass pane. An old gentleman in white cotton shorts on his morning walk turned around and looked at Neema with an amused smile under his big, fat moustache as did the woman next door who had come out to see her little son off to school.

Neema finally dashed inside the house and screamed with tears standing in her eyes, 'Hurry up and remove your car. *You bastard!*' The last two words went inaudible. She had to gulp down and repress from uttering them aloud which otherwise would be an uncalled-for behaviour from a wife still with strings attached. *Perhaps someday her grandchildren would daringly vocalise their inner thoughts.* She waited for Arjun to respond to her calls.

He emerged and began to climb down in a calculated manner, a little smile twitching on his big, wide mouth. He leisurely buttoned the cuffs of his white formal shirt. 'Pugnacious!' He scowled as he walked past her. She followed him, hurriedly holding onto the pleats of her sari, lest she trip over it, and watched him start his car. The puny moustached man who had suddenly appeared at his gate diagonally opposite waved with a grin when Arjun drove his car out of the garage and parked it close to the compound wall. Neema hurried inside the garage and turned on the engine with spiteful anger. She didn't know who the puny man was waving at. All the same, she wanted to butt him in the face. She heard her husband's cool words, 'He is watching your henpecked face,' trail behind her as she drove off.

And ah, now a misogynist principal to deal with at the college! She angrily changed the gear and steered to make a left turn. A cyclist wheeled in from nowhere and zoomed past her. She jammed her foot on the brake and her car came to a screeching halt while the signal light turned to red. Those Dunlop tyres had moved past the zebra crossing. A dark, well-built policeman left his spot and walked towards her, whistling, with a book and pen in his hand. She tried to argue with him, saying that it was the cyclist's mistake, but she was not spared. A receipt with the fine amount scribbled in was shoved into her palm. Fighting back her tears, she gave him the money and drove onward. Traffic rules were not mandatory for cyclists in India, she rued. The thought jabbed through her mind with remorse.

Adding to her disappointment, anger, and some kind of deep sadness, her mother's repulsive words bounced back in her head, bringing forth in stark reality her mother's attitude towards her and a strange fondness for Arjun.

An excellent husband who gulps down your temper, manages domestic chores, and still has earned a reputation as a successful lawyer. Gem of a person!

She had said that more than a dozen times in all those eight years of Neema's marriage.

Neema cranked up the tinted front windows with bitterness, wore her dark sunglasses, turned on the air conditioning and the music player. It was such a relief. It felt good to hide her puckered face from the world.

The third traffic signal light! She rapped the steering wheel restlessly with her fingers. The countdown timer signaled the remaining five seconds. The red numerals were still rolling down. Vehicles that had lined up behind had already started to honk crazily, as if those in the front row were leisurely daydreaming with nothing better to do. Her heart raced faster with the stupid honking and when those behind her zoomed past as if in a race, she dropped her jaw with annoyed amusement for once again swinging to the road on her right became difficult. However, the cool temperature inside her Maruti 1000 and Eminem's rap were the relieving anodynes that helped her compete with the remaining ongoing traffic rushing madly alongside hers.

Once inside her college campus and with her car safely parked, she felt happy as always, with a bubbly cheerfulness on her face. The sight of those youngsters always lifted up her drooping mood. It was with earnestness and ardour that they attended her classes, and she was equally keen on grilling them with life's skills besides the mandatory syllabus. She loved her students and her career. It was her job that gave some succour to her otherwise charmless life.

Now, when she nimbly walked into the staffroom, to her great relief, she found the staff attendance register still lying on her bare wooden desk. Rumour had it that in about five years' time, the college would introduce swiping machines to record staff attendance. Well, that would be 1995, when her daughter would be on the threshold of her teen years! Neema smiled to herself as she signed in the log book, imagining the day when the staff would be vying with each other to swipe the machine in precedence. *A long way to go!* She sighed and slumped on her office chair.

In that dusty, musty, cob webbed government staff room sat a male colleague scanning a vernacular newspaper, his face hidden behind the sheets. A brief, absentminded smile and a faint 'Hello' greeted her from his dusty table. He callously remarked from behind the sheets, 'A new principal has taken charge.'

Neema flashed a smile in acknowledgement, but he was still hidden behind the newspaper. He finally stood up, stretched himself to the accompaniment of a wide, audible yawn, neatly folded the newspaper, put it aside, picked up his duster along with a few chalk pieces, and made his exit.

Neema was amused to watch the impassivity that the avocation had brought upon him. After he left, she sat and stared out the window, ruminating over the years of her career as a teacher there. The work environment had remained the same in spite of the role of principals being grabbed by several characters–dramatis personae. Each had brought in his own rule, but had never succeeded in bringing to his office the reputation that carried him into it. The period of each of them was as short as his predecessors and his moments of ecstasy were ransomed by years of hatred. It was the same story with the heads of the various departments. Only by virtue of one's seniority did one sit in that exclusive chair. No other criterion was held as a benchmark to promote him or her to that authoritative post. Each expressed his or her authority in ludicrous ways that were gender or knowledge biased.

Undoubtedly, it was Masculine power that reigned supreme. The narrow-minded, small vernacular worlds in which the majority of the government employees were brought up seemed to have stymied their ability to look at things from a broader perspective. Someone smarter than themselves was viewed as a threat. Teachers who became students' favourites were envied. The workplace held no promise of progress. Nobody trusted anybody; everybody remained an island in the flux of hundreds of employees, and somebody was always there to pull down another's enthusiasm and zap his propensity to favour pedagogy or the student community.

Neither was the faculty spared from accusations and nasty remarks from the so-called higher-ups and were many times made to run not just from pillar to post but to the next station as well to pursue small matters like the settlement of one's remaining leave of absence or pending salary of foregone months or other increments. It was ludicrous. The pseudo-educated officers of the pay or administrative department were a set of surly bullies who misplaced records or misinterpreted or simply stanched communication and used tones that peaked towards altercation. It was not a place for the frail and sensitive. Yet she had survived for over a decade, and she acknowledged this with a small smile to herself. That was incredible! There were attitudes and mannerisms aplenty to deal with. She sighed deeply and turned her head back to her table. Within moments, she too picked up her books, duster, and chalk, and left.

While Neema was on her way back to the staff room, having finished her class, Pada, her only close friend in her workplace, one who taught in the commerce department, caught up with her in glee. 'I finished my class too,' she smiled. 'But before we head to the canteen, let me first tell you what happened in my class.' She was giggling through her words.

Pada always had one or the other funny incident to narrate, and that kept Neema pleasantly occupied during her spare time. What held them together was their propensity to laugh in good humour over trivial things.

That was how Neema had been even as a student. Her wit and sense of humour evoked funny images over which she and her friends would always have a hearty laugh.

Now the two headed towards Neema's staff room while Pada prattled on with bursts of laughter at the absurdity of what had happened to her an hour ago.

'Know what?' She tried to put on a long face. 'My long gold chain with the mangalsutra snipped off while I was teaching before all those boys and girls,' she repined through snickering laughter.

While Pada narrated the incident, gesticulating with a flushed face, the two tarried in the corridor and Pada continued, 'I turned around from the blackboard to the students, lowering my hand at the same time, and the duster got stuck in my long chain. It was so embarrassing. It got looped around the duster and when I twirled the chain and tried to pull it free, it broke and the black beads rolled under all the desks, and you must have seen the look on the students' faces!' she said in a single breath. Neema was shaking with laughter. By the time they pulled out their chairs, they could only plonk down, for they were laughing their guts out.

Neema could imagine her friend's goofus plight with her tiny paunch hidden behind the pleats of her sari and she tugging at the duster through the loops of the encircled mangalsutra.

She finally remarked, wiping her nose with her little handkerchief, 'That's funny! The students would have thought of you as a messy teacher.'

'Shall we please go to the goldsmith?' Pada asked beseechingly with her ruddy face, smacking her dry lips with her tongue.

'Is it so important?' Neema narrowed her eyes teasingly.

Pada, still simpering with a flushed face, turned around to see whether the two male lecturers who were seated at the far end were overhearing them, and after being convinced that they were involved in their own heated discussion about last night's cricket match, bent forward and whispered with a degree of supposed seriousness, 'Know what? You know the things people comment when they notice us not wearing mangalsutra. We must wear it for the sake of others. That is how our country is!' she declared, straightening up. They giggled again silently.

'Look,' Neema said eventually, bringing out her own mangalsutra chain from the folds of her sari. Raising it with her thumb, she asked, pointing at the two little gold plates with their tiny gold beads at the centre, 'Tell me what they look like.' There was a certain degree of confrontation in her merry tone.

'What's special about them?' asked Pada inquisitively, failing to grasp the implication.

'Tell me what they look like? Are they not symbolic of ladies' breasts? Look at these tiny balls right at the centre of the two small convex gold plates.'

Pada broke into hysterical laughter and made a great effort to mute it by bending her head over her arms on the table, while Neema with her palms on her own bemused mouth waited for her friend to compose herself.

Finally when Pada lifted her flushed face, she managed to say with forced decorum through an erupting cough and tearful eyes, 'Nobody has ever told me anything like this! Moreover, all Indian women do not wear mangalsutras of the same type.'

'Men wear nothing symbolic to indicate they are married. Do they?' Neema spoke with a kind of prodding resentment as she stood up. Pada arched her eyebrows in supposition and shrugged her shoulders, reflecting over it. They finally headed towards the canteen for their favourite cup of coffee and drove to a goldsmith in the market area.

After they got back from the goldsmith, Neema went into the staff room. Her male colleagues were grading some test papers. What was ostensibly a smile, curled her lips as she sat there watching them. The dream that troubled her night after night haunted her, surfacing from the dark crevices of her mind, where she secretly bore an unpardonable hatred for the man who had married her with no intention of treating her as his wife. He had tied the mangalsutra and taken vows before the sacred fire in the presence of hundreds of people who had gathered in the embellished, palatial choultry on that rainy Christmas day; it had cost her dad his fortune trying to please every wish of those in-laws who spoke butter cookie words and said in private that it cost them nothing to dole out such words.

Her mom's perennial apathy towards her was the primary reason, she had felt, that had driven her to commit herself to a lifelong relationship to a man she knew nothing about, and it had crumbled to dust even before the dust of her baby's feet could bring her life's eternal joy. Her loving dad's brief displeasure towards her for having rejected two earlier proposals had also been the cause for her eventual decision. And above all, it was Arjun's impressive green eyes that had made her hold on to her decision unwaveringly, in spite of her aunt's taunting remark that he was already going bald.

Glancing towards her, a male colleague suddenly passed a comment, which sounded more like a question, 'Madam seems to be pondering over something.'

'No,' she denied it promptly, straightening herself. 'Just watching you guys go about your work so seriously.'

'Many here call you a bubbly girl,' one of them said.

She flashed a big smile and got up to leave, gathering her handbag.

'I'm so glad it is Sunday tomorrow,' she added, looking at him and trying to be cheerful.

'You are a happy-go-lucky person. Aren't you?' The two middle-aged guys spoke almost in unison grinning and looking at her as she reached the door.

'Yes, I am,' she replied and left.

CHAPTER THREE

It was breezy outside. With winter round the corner, a late-November grey evening sky greeted her with rain clouds hanging in the horizon. Flakes of silvery, cool, and shimmering sky fringed the thick, dark masses of thunderous clouds. Neema walked towards the parking lot. Her seven-year-old daughter, Goldie, whom she had missed intensely for the past three days, had to be picked up. She hurried to her car and reversed the gear. As she drove, reflective thoughts began to occupy her mind.

The year before, Goldie had been admitted to one of the best private schools in the city, not far from home, where children spoke even with their parents in English, in their drawling Indian accent! Neema always found that weird because it was her conviction that to speak in a foreign language within a family would steal away much of the warmth and intimacy that could be established through one's own language.

Neema preferred to throw her warmth in her vernacular language. And if at all a light, brief conversation ensued between her and another waiting parent, she was always proud to reveal the fact that she was an English lecturer and was amused to see that the listening parent, somehow, would avoid using the English language in her hearing range after knowing this.

Teachers assigned kids a lot of homework, yet Neema saw no reason to deny Goldie the pleasure of spending time with her grandparents. It gave her immense pleasure to hear her kid squeak elatedly, 'Grandpa took me out and bought me gems.' Goldie loved those colourful Cadbury chocolate buttons.

Goldie's happiness was Neema's perennial concern. To be loved and entertained by someone you could call your own, to feel the warmth of someone you could trust from your own family circle, to immerse in joy without any scruples under the affectionate care of someone who shared your blood and gene was the happiest thing on earth. Neema would always ruminate over such things whenever she sent Goldie packing to her grandparents. As such, she never denied Goldie her longing to be with them, although she knew her mother's grand-parenting desire was not something she could count on.

The ten-mile drive to Rajajinagar from her workplace was really tedious and annoying. She shifted the gears with resentment, but stopping by Arya Bhavan to buy sweets for her loving dad was never irksome. Her mom never liked sweets. Neither was she sweet by nature. Though it was difficult to please her, Neema always made it a point to carry some spicy snacks for her. Fruits which she carefully picked always supplemented the short eats.

The narrow, gravelled lane she turned onto corroborated with the painful memories that came flooding in as she drove in the feathery light drizzle, squinting her eyes at the white, soft rays that gleamed on the windshield from a cold sky. Incidents from the past reared their heads again reminding her of old bickering and hard-to-bury, bitter feelings. It was so hard to bury them as quondam stuff, as these visits to her mom's place unfurled as in a palimpsest those die hard memories.

She remembered the day when her mom's dislike for her had brought things to a boiling point, making her furious and strengthening her assumption that the woman, undoubtedly, was her stepmother, although it wasn't true. Even after ten-and-a-half years, Neema could feel the bitterness of it all. The pain and humiliation she had suffered was something she could never forget in her life.

She could remember it all like it had happened yesterday. Mili, her younger sister, had no right to go through her cupboard. But she had done it daringly. Neema had just returned from her friend's house, effervescent and in a joyful mood. However, when she entered her room, she found her locked almirah half-open. None but her sister, who was lying supine on the bed across from the almirah, could have done this.

Neema turned to her with a scowl and questioned sternly, 'Why have you opened my almirah?'

'I needed to look for my panties and bra,' replied Mili with equal sternness without lifting her eyes from the magazine she was pretending to browse.

Neema's ironed clothes were crumpled and her other dresses that had been neatly piled up were disarrayed.

Some of her hangers were lying on the bed, and her white sweater had fresh coffee stains on it. It enraged her like nothing else could. The sweater was her loving dad's birthday present, given to her when she had turned twenty the previous year. It now stared her in the face with long lines of coffee stains, and that was unpardonable.

Neema's immediate instinct was to rush and slap her sister, but instead she stood fixed to the ground, trying to allay her burning rage. Mili was Mom's favourite and the fact that she would get the better of it was unmistakable.

'Why coffee stains on my white sweater? You know Dad will be upset if he comes to know about this,' she growled.

Mili lifted up her angry face and shot a glaring look at Neema. 'I had coffee in my hand,' she hissed.

'Why did you think your panty would be in my cupboard?' Neema barked with distended nostrils and fire burning in her eyes.

'Dad will give you more presents. So what?' The bitter sarcasm in Mili's tone could not be missed as her eyes returned to the magazine.

Neema wanted to wrench her hair. 'You are a dirty mannerless bitch!' she shot back and turned to her sartorial mess.

Mili's sudden scream shot through the air. She leapt out of the bed and flung the magazine at the doorway. Neema instantly guessed why she did so.

Kanthi, their mother, who had been watering the plants in the front yard, dashed into the room like a bolt out of the blue and struck Neema on the face with intense fury.

'Mili is your younger sister. She is three years younger to you,' she screamed with fury. Neema was dumbstruck. Her mom had not bothered to find out the truth; instead, tugging Mili by the arm, she walked out saying, 'How many times have I told you not to get entangled with that girl! Just don't talk to her.'

Neema heard her mom's unbelievable advice doled out affectionately to her pet daughter. The yellow incandescent bulb burned dully in her room, corresponding with the silent, darkening dusk that had fallen outside. This dying sunlight was always the period of the day that brought some kind of hollowness in Neema's chest. It smothered her like a person under water not knowing how to swim. She stood still and pale, as darkness closed in to settle in a pulsating quietude. The night was silent. Neema stood motionless for a long time, leaning against the wall, snuffed with a burning cheek.

Those red stripes on her beautiful, tawny skin had taken two days to clear and the indelible emotional pain and humiliation she had suffered on that day had only furthered her rift with her mom.

She now pulled the car in front of her parents' house, dabbed her eyes before she got out. The huge metal gate was half-open and so was the main door. Goldie was already on the threshold, excited and happy to see her mom. Her ears couldn't miss the sound of her mama's car. Her arms flew around Neema's hips even before she could step into the hall. Kanthi came out of the kitchen with a napkin on her shoulder and gave a twitch of a smile before she clumped to the couch.

Neema handed over the packets gently. 'Hope the apples are sweet, Mother,' she said with a small, conscious smile and started to gather Goldie's clothes and books that were lying jumbled up around the room.

'I can't trouble myself whenever you come,' her mom had once told her with a vexed expression. 'Even if you yourself make coffee, I'll have to clean the countertop again after you leave. There will be coffee stains everywhere.'

Hurriedly collecting Goldie's belongings, Neema prepared to leave.

Kanthi saw them off at the gate. While Neema turned the key in her car, she caught that cynical smile blooming on her mother's face as she stood at the gate, adjusting her well-combed little bun at the back of her head.

Neema strapped Goldie to the seat beside hers and zoomed off. Although there was nothing strange about her mom's attitude towards her, somewhere deep down, she felt perturbed and sad. In an effort to overcome her blue and also to cheer up her daughter, who was sitting rather gloomily, Neema began to narrate the dream that she had seen many years ago that alluded to her mom's demeanour.

She had narrated the same dream to her little group of intimate friends on the campus years ago, and it had sparked off fits of rib aching laughter. She now recalled every bit of it to entertain Goldie.

'Once I had a dream, honey,' she began. Goldie turned and fixed her soft, large, beautiful eyes on her mama and waited to listen.

'Once I had a dream, many years ago, in which your grandmother looked very, very huge.' Neema sighed.

'As huge as a giantess?' Goldie asked with a sudden spark of bubbliness.

'Hmm, almost,' Neema replied, trying to focus on the traffic-ridden road.

Goldie's little plump hand flew to her mouth in giggles. Neema continued with the story.

'Your grandma was frying pooris in the kitchen and tossing them into a colander that was already filled with a mountain of them. Golden coloured, huge, puffed-up ones. I was waiting patiently in the doorway of the kitchen with the plate in my hand for my mom to serve me those delicious pooris. She never turned my side.'

Neema went on in a singsong manner, giving it a dramatic effect to make it sound interesting.

Goldie listened excitedly.

'Suddenly, a poori jumps out of the container and starts chasing me. I scream and fly out of the kitchen. It is hot on my heels. I run around the teapoy and jump up on the couch. The poori hobbles and looks up at me and is mutely muttering something with its fish-like mouth. I really couldn't make out what it was saying,' Neema went on in one breath.

Goldie continued to giggle.

'It had eyes and a mouth?'

'Yeah. Eyes of your grandma and the mouth of a fish.'

Goldie chortled wildly.

'It pursued me unrelentingly. Finally, I hopped onto my bed and there that frantic chase finally came to a halt.'

'How?' Goldie looked at her mama, her mouth puckered.

'It got stuck to the leg of the bed!' Neema simpered.

Goldie giggled all through the way, voicing it in bits, ad libitum. They were near the town hall when the traffic signal flashed its red light. Neema suddenly heard her dad's voice calling out her name from somewhere among the traffic. She craned her neck outside the window, throwing a searching glance amid the traffic. When she turned her head to the other side and peeked through the tinted glass of the backseat, she saw her dad on the sidewalk, hurrying towards them.

'Dad, wait right there. Lemme park the car,' she called out over Goldie's head, gesturing with her palm. Goldie screamed with joy. He waited for them on the pavement among the crowd that flowed from every side while Neema swung the car into the nearby parking lot with difficulty and hurried towards him, clutching Goldie's hand.

He lifted Goldie up and smacked a kiss on each cheek. The kid hung on to him with her little arm around his neck. He looked at his daughter, Neema. 'You could have let her stay with us, sweetheart.' Saying this, he flicked her shoulder and with Goldie in his arms, started crossing the traffic-ridden road. Neema hurried after him understandingly. They walked into a brightly lit, upscale restaurant. They placed their order and sat happily.

'Tomorrow is Sunday. I'll take Goldie back,' Dad said. 'I want you to enjoy your Sunday.'

'With who?' Neema suddenly popped out the question with a subtle frown, though she was aware of what her dad meant.

'Enjoy with your husband, honey,' he said firmly. 'What do you mean with whom?'

'I have told you many times, Dad.' She opened a bottle of mineral water restlessly and continued, a little annoyed, pouring herself a glass of water. 'He never stays at home. He is not that type, you know,' she said, lifting the glass to her mouth.

Gulab jamoon and masala dosa arrived. Dad began to pamper and spoon feed Goldie, who was sitting beside him, excitedly kicking her legs back and forth.

'You are a woman,' he told Neema as he munched. 'You must learn to draw your husband to your side. He is not a bad man after all.'

Neema didn't answer. He looked at her once, briefly lifting his eyes from his plate. She was nibbling, looking at her plate. A frown sat on her brow, her mouth drawn tightly. He sipped some water, cleared his throat, and said affectionately, 'Sweetheart, marriages are made in Heaven. You must save your marriage.' She knew what he intended. He wanted her to be happy. She was young and inexperienced from his perspective, so his purpose was to try to make her see things with his well-meant advice. 'Try hard to please him,' he said quietly, beckoning the waiter. Neema's eyes smarted with unshed tears as she turned in the direction of the waiter. *Please, Dad. I've done that a million times.* The words ran desperately in her mind.

While they sipped coffee, her mind raced through the humiliating incident that she had faced a few years before. She was so bereft of hugs and sex. Her body had begun to crave it. She wanted to be enveloped in masculine warmth, preferring actually a good, hard squeeze to relieve her of the muscular pains she had developed. She knew that other women in her situation would have entered into an extra-marital relationship. But she didn't believe in such a relationship meant only for sex, that had no roots. She believed in the institution of marriage and desired to make it work. But his continuous rejection of her, unwillingness even to hug her or present her with anything that a woman so much desired from a lover, had dashed all her hopes of making her marriage work. Even her desire for him had died down.

That bitter incident on a Sunday afternoon was unforgettable and unpardonable. Arjun was loading the washing machine with his clothes. He had not spoken a word ever since they had woken up, although Goldie was not there to keep them busy. She was with her grandparents. Neema had dreams and desires of seizing such occasions for making love and playing the fool, young and mischievous as she was, and she found his silence very strange. Earlier, on many occasions, she had tweaked his moustache or raised herself on her toes to plant a kiss on his cheek, but he had never responded. In spite of it, she made an effort to humour him, despite his sombre attitude and deadpan look. She lovingly offered to help him by bringing him the bucket and hangers. But he had kicked it aside irksomely and had carried the clothes in his hands. He had maintained his silence and a despicable, grim countenance. She had begun to laugh over his seriousness. And when she had put her arms around his neck, he had simply plucked them off, extricating himself, and had walked away from her. She had followed him undeterred, held him by the wrist with the sweetest possible smile, and lain on his bed, humming a Bollywood song. He had pulled himself free, had started to dress up, and had appeared to be in a contemplative mood, or rather in his own made-up world. She had hopped out and implored him to stay back, promising to prepare his favourite dishes. He had pushed her aside and walked out, slamming the door behind him. She had lain on the bed, sick, the whole day, hugging a pillow, shocked and humiliated, lonely and desperate.

When her dad was paying the bill, Neema hurriedly pulled out a tissue from the tissue container, wiped her running nose, and blinked rapidly to brush away the film of tears that had risen to her eyes. Without lifting her gaze towards her dad, she smiled at Goldie, who was crazily smacking the sugar syrup on her lips.

She offered to drop Dad home, but he flatly rejected. He wanted Neema to reach her home safely, for it had started to drizzle and it was his conviction that rain begun in the late evening would lash ceaselessly, all through the night, never stopping till morn. He assured her that he would drop Goldie at school on Monday morning.

'I take pleasure in it, honey. It's no trouble at all,' he convinced her and added, 'just go home and enjoy with Arjun.' He was incognizant to her inner struggle.

He hired an auto and took Goldie back with him.

CHAPTER FOUR

Darkness was closing in and the ominous weather that was threatening all day suddenly unleashed its demonic pour just when Neema was halfway to her house. Her dad was right. The heavy downpour intensified with the growing darkness.

'Poor dad,' she heaved a deep sigh. She could remember the joy that had lit his face when mom had disclosed that she had chosen an excellent match for his favourite daughter, Neema — a lawyer from a rich family.

Trying to push aside the thought she tightened her grip on the steering wheel and drove on. Streets flooded and gutters overflowed with gurgling brown water, making it impossible for Neema to drive with her usual speed of twenty per hour. She kept peering hard through the windscreen at the dark roads in the lambasting rain, wondering what Goldie would be doing with her grandparents.

Finally, she pulled in front of the huge, ornamental black gate. Meek lights from the row of houses on either side glowed dully and gloomily. Her beautiful mansion, all hushed and enchanting in the blinding rain of late night had its front hall suffused with the glow of the yellow neon bulb that Neema had switched on in the morning. The red-tiled sloping roof projected over the pretty bay window of the living room and the white, frilled lace curtain rippled gently behind the glass, tipping off the solitudinous.

A romantic exterior! Neema sighed with a sad smile. Turning off the engine outside the gate, she scuttled to the porch, groped for the keyhole in the darkness, and finally stepped inside her warm abode, greatly relieved to be inside. Thunder rattled and the sound of the heavy downpour outside intensified. With another deafening roll of thunder, the house suddenly plunged into darkness. And so had the entire street, undoubtedly, which Neema was sure of. The transformers always burst, indubitably, with a downpour of that kind.

All alone that eerie pluvial night, she quickly grabbed a thin, long white candle from the top of the fridge, groped for the lighter, and shakily lit the gas burner and brought out a little dancing blue flame in the cold, dark kitchen before trotting to her bedroom like a fraidy cat. It was not long before she changed into her pink silk gown and jumped into her bed.

A sudden stroke of lightning flashed through the window in a zippy blast, illuminating with its blue luminescence her charming apparition reflected in the long glass pane of the casement window. Simultaneously, the land line telephone in the huge dining hall jarred into life with its sharp ringing. Neema swung her head with a start towards the door. Staring out into the dark hall with her wide eyes, she let it ring ... *Perhaps a client wanting to seek Arjun's legal advice,* she reasoned ... *And, if it was Goldie from Granny's house ... Well, she was safe.* But right then, effete and scared, she did not have the guts to go into the dark hall. A few minutes later, Neema skidded under the satin razai and dozed off under the lull of the incessant rap of the rain outside.

Her buried thoughts resurfaced and began to roll into a nightmare again.

A ghost like image of herself roaming the wild woods and thrashing him insensibly under a moonless, velvety sky. Zigzag of fiery lightning revealing monstrous aerial shoots of the huge banyan tree that dangled like famished ghosts in the creepy night.

With a glint in her eyes, she stood between the trees in a long white shirt and watched the vanquished man with vengeful hatred and listened with cruel delight to his tortured breath under the aerial roots, heavy in the silence like the dying moan of a slayed Kamsa. Blood streaked from a corner of his mouth. Gory in the tempestuous darkness of dusty stars, weakly peeking into the obsidian vault. Pure delirium! A burning vindication!

His green eyeballs floated like marbles in pools of watery eyes before they fixed themselves upon her in a cadaverous stare and all that she could see in the pitch dark was his pair of grim, revengeful green eyes in his ferocious countenance like that of a wild cat's in the darkness of a thick jungle. But he was tied, helpless, and vanquished. She drew in a deep breath with a subtle smile—a mocking gesture. Her stifled spirit, at last emancipated from the clutches of emotional torture, joyed in its newfound courage.

She jolted from her sleep in the dead of night breathing hard, her brow moist with sweat. It took a few moments before she realised that she was alone in the huge house. She stared into the lucid darkness of her room with a dry throat, a parched throat that actually should have been the prerogative of the lone dog outside on the silent, wet streets creating a threnody to her nightmare that was sinister in nature and hideous in its call.

Neema pushed aside the light blue satin razai and turned in her bed, feeling somnolent and dopey and warm in spite of the cool breeze wafting in from the half-open window. The incubus gone, she raised herself on her elbow and reached for the bottle of water on the bedside table. As she did so, her gaze slowly moved involuntarily to the white marble stairway that voluted and rose majestically at the farther end of the silent hall outside, faintly visible by the dull ochre glow of the solitary night lamp in the corner that was game to the revived electric current. The dead generator in its dark, deep space looked like a crouching tiger in the dull light of the lamp. The lamp itself was a pretty brass piece with a brawny umbrella that cast obscure, dark shadows of the rosewood banister and the long S-shaped metal balusters —shadows that winced like ghouls on the ice cold vitrified cream floor.

She put back the half-emptied bottle in its place, turned, and rolled in the bed again and lay on her tummy dispassionately, with her arms tucked under her temple, and stared dully into the dark, chill void of her room through her half-open melancholic eyes, summoning her dream with a twitch of a pallid smile.

A dream that was horrendous, yet palliative; disturbing, yet narcotic. The house was empty. Arjun didn't return that night, either. And she knew she would never tell that to her father. He would never understand. On the other hand, perhaps he would hold her responsible for not making him comfortable and happy at home.

Goldie would have a fun Sunday. Neema sat in bed and glanced at the round steel clock on the bedside table. In another hour, Sunday's aurora would break and her dad would presume that she would be having fun with Arjun. She climbed out of bed for an early cup of coffee and sighed silently, *so be it!*

CHAPTER FIVE

Arjun was with his friend, Shravana, in Srinagar, a suburb of Bangalore, for their usual nocturnal caper in the small, dinky bachelor house that they had rented on the first floor of an old, abandoned building that was once a lawyer's office. Priya and Tara had already showed up. Now, it was not necessary to make a booty call for them. They were already sitting half-naked on the bed on either side of Shravana, sipping rum, puffing cigarettes, and running their long fingers with painted nails on his hairy chest. An array of condiments and liquor bottles occupied the wooden table that was placed against the wall.

Though Shravana was shorter than Arjun by almost a foot, he was brawnier. He pulled out another cigarette, stuck it between his lips, and allowed his secretary, Tara to flick the lighter for him. As she did so, she let her boobs touch his hands liberally and smiled at him before she casually pecked him on the cheek. He let her take a drag and passed the packet to Arjun, who had thrown himself comfortably on the recliner below the bookcase. Arjun lit a cigarette, took a long drag, and lifted up his chin in deep, reflective relaxation, letting the smoke curl up in the air, pouting his thick, slimy lips and closing his eyes to feel the kick of it. He pulled Priya onto his lap, and the brunette sprawled with her bare legs on either side of his hip. Her shorts and bra were her only clothing and Arjun always liked her that way before he stripped her even of that in bed.

Shravana opened his eyes and drawled blissfully, looking in the direction of Arjun, 'You are the luckiest guy in the world.' He paused, with drunken eyes mischievously watching the curl of smoke snaking in the air. 'A supportive mother-in-law, a wife who never questions, a free life enjoying here.' He could not hold back his gurgling laughter, for he had said it with intentional sarcasm. However, he meant no offence or harm, for such was their long-lasting bond. Somehow, it sounded so funny to his own ears that he gave a hearty laugh and took another sip of the rum.

The dingy room was filled with smoke. Clothes and undergarments belonging to Shravana and the girls were piled on the wooden stand next to the table. Arjun held Priya's boobs and pulled her closer to him. Finally, he undressed and said that he would stay the night. The girls shrieked and began to rock their hips. Shravana telephoned a nearby restaurant and placed an order for four. They huddled together on the double bed and rolled on each other's naked bodies with transcendental pleasure.

Arjun had always been a hostel resident. His hometown, Hassan, district headquarters with a population of less than ten lakh, hardly had any good centres of education. At Bangalore, he had struck a wonderful friendship with his hostel roommate, Shravana, who was doing an engineering course. Their friendship had turned into a mysterious relationship. Their independence and carefree lives had ultimately turned them into bisexuals. They not only enjoyed each other's company, they enjoyed girls, too. And now, with their well-settled jobs, they had permanently hired Tara and Priya as their office secretaries, girls who with utmost readiness and joy had donned their roles with élan.

Making love with each other's naked bodies as a foursome was something they looked forward to almost every weekend. On other days, they either met in a social club over a drink or it was just the male duo who met for a game of cards or billiards over unlimited liquor.

Arjun, now after going limp stared deep into his girlfriend's eyes, rather soberly, his mouth puckered and hands locked under his head. He mused secretly in his dirty brain as to when he would inherit the thirty acres of productive coffee plantation from her father, Dasappa. It thrived in Madikeri, running to crores of rupees.

Luxuriously independent in Bangalore, he had become a victim of Satyr and Mammon and had set his eyes on Priya's wealth, knowing fully well that she was the only daughter of a wealthy estate owner. *Hadn't she spent a lakh just for his birthday?* He mused.

A year and a half had passed since then. As she belonged to a caste that wasn't acceptable by Brahmins, he had kept his marriage at bay, much to the displeasure of his aging parents. Marrying Neema nine years ago, which then had seemed convenient, had now put him into a hapless situation, for without divorcing her, he could not enter into another legal marital bond. Shravana had advised him not to take the first step in divorcing Neema.

Suddenly furious with the thoughts, Arjun took a deep breath and pushed Priya off his bare chest. She who was already dozing over him gave out a loud snore and rolled close to her friend, Tara, who was deeply asleep in the arms of Shravana.

Arjun sat on the edge of the bed, swinging his hairy legs. With his palms pressed on the bed on either side, he deeply contemplated on the things that had happened in the recent past. Just three months ago, to strengthen his bond with Priya's family, he had unscrupulously joined hands with Dasappa in murdering Priya's uncle, Dasappa's younger brother. He had stood and watched slyly the unsuspecting heavily built man eat the poisoned festival food in his brother, Dasappa's house and die like king Duncan in Macbeth. He further helped Dassappa get fake property documents, transferring the dead brother's forty-acre rubber plantation to his name. He slowly turned and looked at Priya in the faint light of the tiny night bulb. She had fallen asleep.

Their relationship had gone steady, yet they had not been able to marry because of Neema, who he had thought would leave him! The meaningless pompous marriage had taken place as per his parents' wishes. Kanthi had played the role of prime charlatan in their marriage. With this secret up his sleeve, Arjun had felt safe and liberated to continue with his dark life. In spite of neglecting Neema, she had not walked out of marriage. *She was an idiotic bitch!* He spat into the washbasin and started to comb his hair with the first rays of dawn. He had not gone home for four days. The three-day Madikeri trip with Priya had done him good, and the fourth night too, he was here, not wanting to go home. But he needed fresh clothes. He gathered his vesture and began to get dressed.

Shravana partly opened his heavy eyelids and croaked with a crinkled face, 'Go in the evening, bastard.' He went back to sleep, turning his other side towards the wall.

Priya too was stirred from her sleep. She offered to prepare coffee for Arjun. She brought-two cups of hot instant coffee and sat on the plastic chair against the wall and watched him sip sitting on the edge of the bed absorbed in his own thoughts in the silent, partial darkness of the room.

She recalled with pleasure the previous night's enjoyment and the blissful moan she had succumbed to. She had dozed off on him, his hardness having gone limp. She started to giggle with coffee shaking in her hand. She saw him mimic her, place the cup on the floor and lie back with his hands locked under his head.

Slowly sipping her coffee, she silently reflected upon her past life and recalled the sex that she had with a professor while at law school. He had come out so quick that she had lain beside him, silently cursing him.

Back in Madikeri, her native town, she had been in love with Kiran, two years her senior at school. As long-time residents of the same small town and as students of the same school, their friendship had blossomed into love.

Kiran had passionately promised to marry Priya that wet, cold, dreary Sunday evening when they had hopped into a church to seek refuge from the sudden downpour. But after their graduation, they had taken their different ways. She had rushed to Bangalore to enrol herself for a five-year law course while he had taken an express train to Mumbai to join the much sought-after medical course.

While at law school in Bangalore, she had foolishly fallen in love with a professor twenty years her senior and had been impregnated by him in one of their drunken moods when actually she had begun to think of quitting him. She had wept and begged her parents to forgive her and they, who knew about her love for Kiran, protected and defended her with equanimity. Her father, Dasappa, rushed her to a maternity hospital in Bangalore, helped her get an abortion, and encouraged her to resume her studies.

After six years, Kiran had returned to Madikeri to practise as a doctor, whereas Priya, unfortunately, could never succeed in completing her law course.

Dasappa's household servant, who had become intimate with the doctor, often receiving free medical treatment without any scruples, had let the cat out of the bag one chilly evening. He told Kiran all about Priya's abortion and her truant lifestyle in Bangalore. Kiran, perturbed by the whole thing, instantly decided to marry the girl of his parents' choice.

Three months later on a summer holiday, when Priya dropped by his clinic, he refused point-blank to even meet her. Later, he hastily sent words to her parents through a peon that his marriage had been fixed by his parents and that he had dropped the idea of marrying Priya. As an act of revenge on both Kiran and the professor, Priya had ultimately decided to marry the latter, in spite of the age difference. It was easier for her to threaten him and coax him to divorce his first childless wife and marry her. Their names were entered in a sub-registrar's office in Bangalore and they were declared as husband and wife.

A year after her marriage, at the age of twenty-nine, dissatisfied with her aged husband, she had secretly taken the job of an escort to satisfy her burning physical desire until Arjun and Shravana had begun to booty call her. Tara was another in the lewd business, almost the same age as Priya, invited frequently to their dingy room until the men decided to have the girls as their permanent secretaries.

Priya had begun to entice Arjun with her coquettish charm and expensive gifts, wealthy as she was. She celebrated his birthday with much ado and patiently iced his age, thirty-six, on the cake with butter cream. She even presented him a precious diamond ring and made him cut the three-tier cake. *Hadn't he helped her establish herself as a legal secretary in spite of not having a degree certificate?* And now all that she wanted was to marry him and become his legal wife. She was happy with his strong libido and the occasional encouragement he gave her to attend small court matters. She had sent the birthday photos to her dad in Madikeri, who sensed that she had found her true love. Dasappa was happy for her and had been least interested in knowing Arjun's background.

Placing her cup on the table, she stepped up next to Arjun and smiled with a twinkle in her eyes. His eyes moved to hers. She lay beside him kissing him once again.

CHAPTER SIX

Neema sat in the cold window sill upstairs in Goldie's room, sipping a second cup of coffee that Sunday morning. The chill morning air on the dull grey day suddenly made her shiver and brought goose bumps on her arms. But she loved it. She loved the feeling of the chill wind on her skin. Her naïve dad would be thinking that she was having fun with her husband. The long stretch of hills in the distance looked pale and misty, like black triangular strokes painted by some facile hand.

She lazily walked downstairs, letting her eyes fall on a neglected magazine lying on top of the bookcase. Placing the empty coffee cup on the dining table, she brought the magazine to the table and flipped the pages. A bold heading with the words *sex* and *marriage* caught her attention. 'Sex is an integral part of marriage,' the article read. 'Sex induced by pure and natural love between partners could help in their spiritual development,' it said.

Her mind wandered away from the printed matter. *Let alone sex. There was not even love between her and her husband! What a mockery of her marriage!* The clock on the wall behind her marched quietly ahead with its sing song ticking in the silent house.

Neema looked at the magazine page again through the film of tears that had filled her eyes.

'My mother's arms are always open when I need a hug,' said another tiny write-up as she turned the pages.

Her own mother had flung the nastiest remark years ago. That was another traumatic experience that had her at her wit's end. On her twenty-second birthday—the special day of the year when people around should have been showering their care, love, and blessings!—that joyful day had turned out to be a doomsday for Neema. Her mother's remark had spurred her to the resolution to get married to any guy brought in by her parents.

On that special day, she recalled with pain now, as soon as she woke up, her loving dad had gifted her a tall, cylindrical box that seemed to be full of chocolates, but when Neema excitedly flipped open the lid, a mottled paper snake sprung up, causing her to fling the box with a loud scream. Dad was laughing his wits out. He knew his girl's tendency to laugh over trivial, comical things.

'That's enough! All that laughing and playing out there,' Kanthi, who was preparing breakfast in the kitchen had shrieked. Neema who was laughing intensely suddenly gone pale. She was aware of her mom's dislike for her. She had even heard her blame dad once for not maintaining his propriety with daughters with particular reference to Neema.

'Spilling your love on a grown-up daughter like Neema, who ought to be brought up more soberly for discipline's sake, is something I do not appreciate of. She is the eldest and must cultivate manners, not play and laugh with you like a kid,' she had retorted and dad had condemned her and a small fight had ensued between the two. When Kanthi screamed from the kitchen, Neema had sensed by her tone, that she, certainly, was fuming with hateful thoughts.

Dad actually patted Mili's head in good humour to get her also involved in the fun, but she tried to ward off his hand in anger. She, who had sat on the couch, after a while had marched off into the kitchen with burning eyes.

Jealousy! Neema inferred. And she knew that mother would have exchanged cynical, simpering looks with Mili, who was her favourite daughter for she had seen the two do it once. She heard her mother shriek once again, 'Don't you need breakfast?' Dad hurried to the kitchen with Neema following him.

With his plate of idlis, while dad went to settle on the sofa, Neema waited at the jamb. Kanthi stuck a plate of idlis in front of her, glared, and said with spiteful mockery, 'You have put some spell on Dad, huh? He loves playing with you always.' The words had come piercing like a pike and torn Neema's heart like nothing had. 'What a good pair you make, ha!' her mother had added.

With her head drooped, Neema had turned back and marched into her room. A new plastic bag from a popular boutique with a birthday card pinned to it lay on her bed. With her face crinkled, she neglected it and slouched on the floor with her back against the wall, shocked and humiliated.

Spell on Dad? What was her mother talking about? She sat motionless, staring at the floor with a melange of feelings invading her—anger, grief, hatred, disgust. A lump of inexpressible grief choked her throat and her heart raced in disgust. The woman had mocked Dad's gentleness, his kindness, his affection, and his good humour. If there was one person who loved Neema unconditionally, it was her dad. He had always been defensive of her and was resolute in his fatherly love for her.

Neema's bitter acrimony eventually gave way to audible sobs. Tears flowed freely down her flushed face. She huddled there for a long time, her bare feet tucked in the warmth of her cotton gown. She didn't want to be part of that family anymore. Finally, she pulled herself up with one firm decision. And that was to get married, even if it meant jumping from the frying pan into the fire.

She conjured Milan, her strikingly handsome classmate, and imagined being in his loving arms. She lifted her eyes from the floor and saw a shaft of sunlight slanting down through the lattice window of her shady room. A bright smile possessed her. It was a beam scattered into needles of bright rainbow sparklers. She hopped forward, squatted, and held her palm in it and with childish joy watched in amusement, through the film of tears, her fingers appearing to be thicker and closer to her eyes.

A sudden draught of chill breeze shook her up. She looked out the window. Beyond the overhang, it was bright and sunny outside. Remembering Milan had brought in added stimulation. The tall, fair, handsome guy with his curtained hair, who enjoyed playing pranks with her, was beckoning her to his arms. She stood up and looked at her reflection in the mirror. *A flawless skin, dimpled cheek, impressive eyes, and charming smile! No wonder her mother was jealous of her.*

She turned and felt the plastic bag on the bed, ripped it open, and pulled out a dress and admired the beautiful yellow and orange, hand-embroidered salwar kameez that Dad had bought for her. She held the soft dress against her cheek, kissed it, thanked her dad silently, and got into it. Plaiting her hair, she stepped into the hall and silently touched the feet of her mom and dad, who were sitting opposite each other; Mom flipping the pages of a magazine and Dad attending to his office files.

Her dad verbally blessed her and cupped her cheeks with good-humoured grin, but Mom had remained silent, with only a smile curling up in the corner of her mouth.

Lost in thoughts of the bygone past, Neema climbed down the stairs. Sitting on the huge sofa in the commodious living room all alone, she realised that Sunday had advanced into mid-afternoon. The doorbell rang unexpectedly. She stood upright and looked at herself in the dark glass of the television. Her desire to look fresh and cheerful always made her 'the bubbly girl' to the world, having no worries. She scurried towards the door and opened it. A young, good-looking salesman greeted her and brought some products out of a cloth sling bag. She scanned through the set of educational books and cassettes and casually asked him how many he had sold for the day. Words flowed enthusiastically out of his smiling mouth. He said he had already sold four sets and that he wanted to be back at his office before the sun went down and . . . He prattled on. She was not much listening, but stood smiling out of courtesy and the need to have someone talking to her at least for a while. Finally, she thanked him and closed the door.

She headed to the kitchen and made herself a cup of tea. Pouring it into her favourite tiny white china cup, she returned to the living room and sat on the couch, staring blankly at the black idiot box. She was not a movie buff nor had any interest in soap operas. Sunday had died down. She had spent it all alone.

She emptied the cup and twiddled it around in torpor, wistfully studying the tiny, motley pairs of ball dancers in sixteenth century attire artistically painted by some facile fingers on the cup's exterior. *So lucky!* She sighed and kissed the tiny images, feeling the warmth of the cup on her lips.

She ran her fingers through her dishevelled hair, stood up, and looked out the window through the white lace curtain. She stood staring into the darkness, as minutes ticked by. Finally tired and sleepy, she blew a flying kiss to the crescent moon that had emerged, and glad that the heavenly object was smiling back at her, she sprawled on the couch turning the pages of a magazine. Minutes later, she heard a click in the keyhole. Uncomfortably, she shifted her position on the couch in the dark living room. Arjun was stealing in. The dull light of the single corner lamp in the inner hall was enough to guide him upstairs. When she heard the door of his room close, she sneaked into her own bedroom silently, curled up, and dozed off and dreamed a dream that she could never forget for a long time in her life.

There she stood, solitary and lost, thrashed by the wind among the stalks of a paddy field. Perplexed and cast away with no destiny or destination. Black clouds rumbled in the medusoid firmament and raced forward in a frenzied force. The sleeve of her white shirt rolled up, she held her arm across her brow against the tempestuous storm. All of a sudden the dark sky split and revealed a gigantic illuminated crater—a shimmering white gorge. A radiant golden chariot was fast approaching in her direction. She could see the mighty Lord Vishnu in dazzling splendour with his conch and discus, radiating energy, peace, joy, and supreme love. She fell on her knees in a hosanna before she was lifted into the chariot by the Lord himself to whisk her away to His divine abode forever.

CHAPTER SEVEN

Monday morning, she hurried through her morning chores as usual, thinking about yet another drab day which would pass by. When she stepped out of the house, she was pleased to feel the brumal sunshine—soft, radiant, white, and cheerfully beautiful—seeping through the leaves of a huge tree just outside her compound wall.

On reaching her college, Neema sauntered to the staff room, dully contemplating on submitting a half-day leave of absence and loitering about in the streets of Malleshwaram, munching a pizza with some ice cream. However, it so happened that an unbelievable pleasant surprise awaited her. When she walked into her staff room, she saw a young gentleman seated at her table with his back to the door. Milan had reached there before the morning rush hour could pick up and was waiting with a faint nervous excitement for Neema, the girl who had always been in his dreams. With nothing more than a friendly hug, they had parted on the university campus, grappling with the unexpressed emotions running deep in them. They were passively passionate about each other.

Milan had never dared to express his love for her, for fear of being rejected, since she had always portrayed herself as a rebellious girl. Neither had Neema found the courage to open up her feelings of love for him for fear of not being able to keep to her promise, as she was tied down by the strict parameters laid down by her orthodox parents. In spite of their reticence, they had delighted in each other's company, as they were deeply aware of the invisible cord of affection that tied them together. It was a bond that made them restless, if they missed seeing each other even for a single day. It had remained a non-vocalised love.

He was now sitting at her table, anticipating his rendezvous with her. Neema walked to her table. She had never expected to see him after so many years! Her repressed scream of joy catapulted him to a hearty laugh, the sound of which she loved to hear. He stood up and held out his hand. 'How are you?' he asked.

Neema, five feet and two inches tall, stood looking up bashfully into his romantic, expressive dark eyes. Irresistibly handsome, tall and athletic, almost five feet and eight inches in height. Milan kept smiling deep into her eyes. His sexy, masculine voice rolled out cheerfully, 'I've a lot to say.'

Her heart began to flutter. 'Milan, I don't believe this!' she stammered and pulled out her chair.

'Believe what?' he mischievously asked.

'Believe that you are here.' She nervously smiled, hid her blush behind her cupped hands, coughed pretentiously, grabbed a sheet of white paper from her cupboard, scribbled a leave note, and rose again, picking up her shoulder bag.

'Of course, Milan! We do have a lot to catch up with. Shall we go to some place where we can . . .'

He took her hand and led her out. Certainly they had a lot to exchange, and the staff room was not the place for it.

They rode on his motorbike to a posh restaurant on Airport Road. Sitting across from him in the scarcely populated, hushed ice cream parlour, a section of the restaurant, she noticed that he had hardly changed in all those years. He was just the same—slim, fair, handsome, tall, and a strong guy with long hair that covered his ears—except that his well-defined, bony wrist looked sexier than before.

'You haven't changed much.' He leaned forward on the table, naughtily smiling at her. She looked at him bashfully, brushing aside the hair on her brow, her large eyes twinkling with irrepressible happiness.

'I've always loved that dimple in the middle of your right cheek,' he remarked and added, 'Tell me, pretty girl, how life has been for you?'

'Good,' was all that she could manage to say through her coyness.

He placed the order and resumed his talk. 'You didn't call me, nor received my calls, although I telephoned several times. Your father picked up the call once and said that you had gone out and the next time I called, it was your sister who told me that you were napping. And I never received a call from you.'

She was listening with her hands on the table. *Her dad had always been orthodox in his views. Not giving her a boy's number was understandable. Her sister? She doing something good for Neema was unimaginable.*

She felt his warm palms close over hers. A rush of emotion made her feel dizzy and her cheeks became pink with the adrenaline spike that she was experiencing behind her charming and composed smile.

Milan noticed it. He noticed the blush that had blossomed on her pretty face.

'I went away to America to pursue my doctorate degree and I missed you a lot, baby,' he said. He held her right wrist and with his other hand caressed her open palm. She could see him become emotional too. He kept his eyes bent low on their interlocked hands, so as not to betray his amative feelings. Neema took a deep breath. She was uncertain about what to say. Somehow, she could feel his love running through her.

She merely looked at him across the table with an understanding smile. The waiter approached with two tubs of vanilla and chocolate double sundaes with orange wafers stuck into the scoops and neatly set them on the table with a generous smile.

'When did you come back from the United States?' she finally managed to ask with a pleasant smile as soon as the waiter left. Two other questions rammed in her head—*Are you married? Do you have any children?*

'What are you doing now, by the way?' she quickly added to brush away those thoughts.

'Eating your favourite ice cream with you,' he smiled playfully and glanced at her. 'I loved you, Neema,' he said, point-blank, suddenly looking into her eyes. A spoonful of ice cream had just reached her mouth when her heart skipped a beat and almost froze.

Oh, she loved him too, but had never expressed it.

She fought with her emotion and tried to look at him, intensely conscious of her sheepish look.

'I didn't get married. I'm not married, Neema,' he said quietly.

Her heart beat faster as she listened. She lowered her eyes to her bowl and fumbled with her mute thoughts as much as she fumbled with her spoon. 'How did you find me now?' she asked meekly, hardly able to find her voice.

With one hand on the table and the other fumbling with the spoon, he continued, 'A year ago, I came back from America for good. My sister, who had come down from London, agreed to spare some time for me. She knew I was desperate to see you. So she went to your parents' house and brought back the news that you were married and settled and working in this college now.'

They looked into each other's eyes. A number of thoughts crossed and jostled in their minds. But it wasn't long before she gave in, voluntarily, to a buoyant giggle. She picked up his spoon jauntily, scooped up some ice cream and put it into his mouth.

'Where are you working now?' she questioned spiritedly.

'You've always been like this. Cheerful and airy in your spirits. I run my own business as an educational consultant.'

'Wow! And you are not married yet?'

'I wanted to meet you before I could do so.'

'Now that you have met me, you can go ahead and marry,' she said. She realised that it sounded rude, but she was always like that whenever she had to fight her tears.

Things are always late. She inhaled deeply, clamped her fingers on his fair, hairy wrist, and said rather kindly, 'Please get married before you get old.' Both started laughing. Milan knew the girl well. He loved her deeply.

'Are you happy with your husband, if I may ask so? Is he good to you?' he asked suddenly.

'Good. He is good,' she blurted out with a condescending smile. *Why was he asking that?*

He guffawed and looked straight at her. 'Good in what? In looks, in his heart, in his profession . . .'

'Good in everything,' she said quietly and shrugged her shoulders, moving her gaze rapidly between him and the table. Suddenly, she felt uncomfortable. She wished that he hadn't asked those questions. She could feel a lump in her throat. She wanted to hold Milan and cry on his chest.

Become a weakling? A laughing stock? Miserable thoughts rumbled in her mind. She was a strong-willed person and could resist her overflowing emotions. She knew that Milan loved her and that she loved him too, but that was years ago, when they were much younger. She had a daughter now to care for. Moreover, as a culture-conscious woman, had she not pinned her hopes on getting her ruined marital life back on track?

As they strolled out, he pulled out a visiting card from his pocket and handed it to her. 'Call me whenever you can,' he said and when he dropped her back at her workplace, he said, looking deep into her eyes, 'Call me, if you are comfortable with it.' He had noticed her impulse to clam up. He put out his right hand to say goodbye. 'Remember, Neema, I'm always there for you,' he said and zoomed off.

She couldn't sleep that night. He had stirred her emotions. She couldn't forget the penetrating look of his romantic eyes. Their eyes were locked with deep emotion when they had shook hands and bid goodbye.

She longed to be with her old time friends again. Post campus, the fourth month had seen her off in marriage. The disheartening tides of Neema's marital life had severed her contact with her little group of intimate friends. The past opened its wings and she saw them all vividly, as if they had all happened, but yesterday. Her mind retraced the bumpy aeons of love and hatred in which she had revelled with fascination and desolation, respectively, with friends and her mom, hopping between two worlds of puzzling tears that spoke of joy and of sorrow—an outer world and an inner world.

More than eight years had passed by. Those merry days of yesteryears as a postgraduate student of English

Literature on the Bangalore University campus were memories of a lifetime.

She, along with Lily, Sneha, and Aparna, would clamber aboard the pink and blue university Omni bus, only to grab the single long seat at the rear, a seat which others loathed. Sitting on the back seat, they animatedly discussed the burning issues of society—male chauvinism, wife beating, injustice caused to women, dowry, rape, and a range of other wild topics that made heads turn, some with cheerful smiles and some with annoyed faces. And Neema's voice always sounded rebellious because most of the time, she would cap off the debate by stressing the equal rights of a woman, the need for a woman to be monetarily independent, and the absolute need for a girl's education.

She had seen her grandma hide, in a mustard caddy, her meagre personal savings out of the money Grandpa gave her for everyday fruits and vegetables. She wouldn't want to do that. She would be an independent woman with her own money, flaunting it without shame.

Thus, Neema had earned the name of being 'a rebellious girl' on the campus. She always found that funny, for the truth always stared at her from her diary in which she had penned, *If only I had the courage to confront my mother . . . if only I had the courage to get out of the house . . . if only I had the courage to express my love for Milan. . . . . . .*

Nevertheless, whenever the bus bumped on an unexpected road hump or veered direction sharply, the girls would scream out loudly and break into hysterical laughter. They enjoyed those bumpy rides with tummy-aching laughter, even when they almost hit the roof. They would cough and look into each other's faces with tears running from their eyes.

The petulant driver would watch them from the mirror and no less enjoyed their screams of joy and chirpy palaver, which motivated him to steer in a way that behoved those youngsters to scream louder with joy. Their gale of laughter out did the prattle of the others on the bus.

Milan never failed to join the girls during lunch. Most of the time, he would sit somewhere on the back bench in the class to steal glances at Neema, who would be seated somewhere on the middle bench. Whenever she turned her head on the pretext of talking to some girl sitting behind her, she would catch him eying her, and the smiles they exchanged spoke much of what they felt for each other.

Now, after so many years, Milan had showed up, bringing back all those past memories.

The cold December night air blew in from the window. She quietly slipped out of her bed and scampered noiselessly to the kitchen. Arjun might be in his room. She was never sure about it. Suddenly, all she wanted was a hot chocolate drink. Goldie, after much excited talk about the time she had spent with her granddad the previous day, had curled up in her bed upstairs, in her own bedroom. As Neema walked back to her bedroom, she caught a yellow strip of light right beneath the dark rosewood door of Arjun's room, which was shut as usual. *So he was home.* She curled up in her bed and dreamt of being with Milan and her friends again.

Sleep had clearly abandoned her. She turned from side to side. She smiled with her eyes closed. She could feel Milan's warm fingers clamp around her wrist. She lay on her tummy and again on her back. She couldn't sleep. She sat up and eventually strolled to the kitchen. She had forgotten all about her chocolate drink and she wanted it now.

Past events marched within as she stirred the sweetened cocoa mix into hot water.

On the final day of their graduation, she and her three close friends had decided to freak out. Two cinemas in succession, a huge buffet lunch, window shopping, and laughing their wits out were the things that had kept them busy the whole day.

That was all in 1980, when she had turned twenty-two. She switched off the light and sat at the oval-shaped, black marble dining counter top and gazed at the half moon outside the window that was bright enough to illuminate the dark kitchen.

After bidding goodbye to Sneha and Aparna, Neema and Lily had hired a rickshaw to get back home. Fortunately, they lived in the same area. However, after getting off at a common point, they were reluctant to part and go home. A fast food parlour was right across the road. They gave a high five and started to cross. Lily said she would have masala puri and Neema said that she would have bhel.

While crossing the traffic-ridden road, Lily had spotted her lanky cousin hovering over some books of a roadside hawker on the opposite pavement. Neema was, however, amusing herself eyeing a portly looking man a few paces away trying to bamboozle the traffic. She thought she saw him wink at her when he turned around and looked at her for a second time. When he turned around again, stepping over the pavement at the same time, he tripped messily and dived straight in between two huge ladies like a Spanish bull, splitting them and throwing them off their balance. The women, in turn, who were happily and leisurely standing and chatting, tumbled over, gasping and shrieking, and hit a wooden cart filled with yellow lemons. The cart slanted, went off balance and tossed the lemons up into the air, scattering them everywhere. The appalled women, who were dumped against the upturned cart, presented a funny picture with outstretched legs, their saris billowing and their hands up in the air to shield their heads from hitting against the cart. The girls' hearts went out for them, but they were seized with irresistible laughter and could do nothing more than watch others rush to the women's rescue. Lily's tall, lean cousin was scanning the sky in bewilderment, for lemons had rained on him from nowhere, but he had caught a few with delight. The book vendor too was looking up wondering where the lemons had come from. The bulky, round-faced man who had caused this mess had vanished and the two girls were still laughing when they approached Lily's cousin, whose head was still lifted towards heaven. Neema was introduced, and he was invited to join them, too. Even as they ate, the lanky guy was trying to impress Neema by cracking jokes and constantly shaking his head to keep the curls off his forehead, while Neema couldn't shake off Milan's face from the back of her mind.

When Neema bid them adieu and headed home, it was with great reluctance.

Home is where my gloom lies, she had written in her diary. Walking through the darkening street, she absent-mindedly watched a little urchin sauntering along the road, kicking at an empty tin, his every step blissful without a worry.

If only I could go away somewhere and never had to go home . . .

To ponder over her sulking thoughts, she sat on the bastion of the blooming park just a few paces away from her home in the dying twilight and watched the joggers below scurrying up the flight of stairs on her side. A few women in the distance at the other end of the park were whisking away their little ones. A beautiful azure strip still hung on the darkening horizon in the distance. *When was the last time her mother had hugged her or even had an affectionate conversation with her?* She brooded over it, but couldn't remember any such precious moment, for there were none.

'Please wash the greens before cutting, Ma, or else it tends to lose its nutrients,' was all that she had said once to her mom, for which she had received a reproachful, vitriolic stare, besides a good scolding.

'You think you are smarter than me?' her mother had shouted and had nagged her for almost half an hour.

Neema got up and walked towards her house, prepared to take all the accusations that would be flung at her by her mother for being late. And it did happen.

It was another passing day of reprehension and tears. Another passing day when Neema stood by the large window of her bedroom and whispered her woes and dreams to the twinkling stars. It was another passing day in Neema's sweet twenties, when actually she longed to be somewhere far away, walking through the sands of time.

CHAPTER EIGHT

It was the summer of 1995.

Her morning class over, Pada rushed into Neema's staffroom, all smiles and elated. After working in Tumkur for over three years, she had sought a transfer back. She excitedly showed Neema her new gold necklace, recently bought by her husband. As usual, the two headed towards the canteen, gabbing and giggling. Somewhere deep within, a tinge of sadness bothered Neema for not having a husband like that to gift things. A batch of teachers had arrived from various parts of the state for the half-yearly evaluation of examination scripts, and the canteen was crowded.

Neema and Pada bought themselves each a plate of lemon rice and coffee and settled on the plastic chairs that were fortunately clean. Neema told her friend everything about Milan and their equivocal love for each other.

'Then why don't you have fun with him? Nothing wrong with that.' Pada avouched.

Neema briskly shook her head. 'I have not maintained any contact with him,' she said. 'I have a daughter and

I'm committed to my marriage.'She sighed. She stared at the bottle of water on the plastic table and sat deeply in reflection, actually immersed in her own thoughts. She finally started to speak slowly and softly, resuming eating her rice, 'I don't care, me wasting away as a straw mannequin. I care more about my daughter's reputation and happiness in society. I would rather not malign my name and become the butt of gossip! I wouldn't want to hear society say, "Like mother, like daughter." I want my daughter to be protected and have a good and safe life. I want her to grow up with dignity and pursue her education without any mental disturbance.'

She was now prodding the last spoon of rice on her plate. Things looked double and hazy through the film of tears that stood in her eyes.

'It is . . .'She hemmed, drank a sip of water, and stealthily patted her eyes to wipe off the tears. Fighting back her tears, she said, though her voice quivered a little, 'It is only for my child's happiness I'm living in the same house. I... er. I feel like a guest living in that house. The property itself is his, my husband, Arjun's. I don't want Goldie to miss a father.' She lifted her eyes towards her friend and gave a pert smile.

An unsolicited voice from behind said, 'You don't like your hushband, do you?'

Neema raised her eyebrows querulously and turned around with a frowning smile. It was that conservative gossipy woman from a small town in Belgaum district of Karnataka, a maths professor.

Mildly shocked, Neema stammered a reply with her head half-turned around. 'I don't know what you are talking about,'

The woman, who could not even pronounce the aspirated consonant, was poking her nose unnecessarily, having gathered half-cooked grains of their conversation by eavesdropping, and her intrusion was unsolicited.

'All that you shaid only means that you don't like your hushband. Do you?' the woman sniggered as she spoke, adjusting her spectacles over her nose. Neema suddenly lost her temper. She almost wanted to punch her in her face, but her reputation and status held her back.

She turned back to Pada and grimly sipped her coffee, trying hard to get pacified. Pada, too, smiled and signalled her to cool down. With all the perturbed emotions and the lonely, loveless life that Neema was dealing with, this woman had daringly popped up with a needless question.

The woman turned back to her own table and her little group of companions, but continued loudly, clearly directed at Neema, 'You were shaying shomething. Sho I thought you don't like your hushband. I'm shorry for talking middle. You two were talking no.'

'Why wouldn't I like my husband?' Neema shot back in a challenging tone without turning around. She was fuming inside with the knowledge that any betrayal of her personal life would create a furore on the campus.

'I've sheen your hushband once,' the woman continued in the same unperturbed, soothing tone. She had now half-turned her head. 'You had invited ush all for your daughter'sh birthday. You remember? He ish a very good man.'

Neema was now angrily biting the corner of her lips and breathing hard.

She abruptly got up to leave, and so did Pada. Before quitting the place, Neema fixed the maths professor with a malicious stare and said with spiteful anger, 'Mind your own business. I don't know what length of time you spent with my husband to know him so well?' She turned and left fuming. She did not miss the stunned look on the maths professor's face. Many had turned their heads to look at the professor.

Pada gathered her purse and left with Neema hot on her heels.

'How could she be so judgmental?' Neema berated on the way. 'How dare she pass comments on my personal life?'

Pada maintained silence. At length, she said, 'I'm sorry about what happened, Neema,' and walked towards her own staff room.

Neema hated her life. She swung her car out of the parking lot and began heading home. A soft, heavenly golden beam shone in the crimson evening sky.

Depression clouded her. She drove recklessly, fighting back emotions that had gathered like stormy clouds within.

Once inside her abode, she threw herself on the bed and lay still for a long time, vacantly, hyperventilating through parched lips. She sensed Goldie climbing up the stairs and after half an hour leave the house again. She was in the seventh grade and a little independent or, rather, was becoming a little secretive.

As the last spatter of evening light faded, Neema sensed that the house was shrouded in twilight darkness.

She got up and stepped into the hall. She switched on the lights and looked around the empty house. She badly needed a cup of steaming coffee.

But she did not walk to the kitchen. She headed to the little pooja room in a corner of the commodious dining hall. She had left its doors open in the morning after lighting the little sacred lamps. She strode into the little room and sprawled on the floor in front of the Krishna idol, who was smiling at her with his bucolic pipe in his hands. Eventually, she exploded in loud uncontrollable sobs until her heaving chest unburdened itself and purged her from the gloom that had swaddled her.

With her face drenched in tears, Neema sat there looking up at Him, overpowered by his gentle and radiant eyes, impuissant by His transcendental glory. With the golden halo made of Plaster of Paris around the back of His head, He stood with His legs crossed, enduringly resplendent in beauty with the celestial glow on His charming, smiling face. A power emanated from his benign smile, numbing her thoughts to nullity. When her restless heart had gradually pacified, she wiped her cheeks, offered Him a pale smile, and fell in obeisance before His divine feet.

Finally, she was up on her feet, seeking her way to the kitchen. She felt relieved to find some coffee decoction in the newly bought coffee maker. Pouring herself a steaming cup, she sat and stared dully out the kitchen window, into the dark, breezy void.

She heard the restrained sound of the door open. The soft voice of Goldie chatting with a friend could be distinctly heard and then the sounds of them climbing up the stairs.

Neema sat in the dark kitchen with the coffee for quite a long time. She had gone through a lot earlier as a girl in her mom's place and was enduring a wretched life even after marriage. How could people pass remarks about another's personal life without having the faintest idea about what lay hidden behind a smiling face? Without a psychological analysis of things and situations, they were inclined to jump to conclusions!

With a sad, helpless smile at the irony of it, Neema recalled Sigmund Freud:'The ethical demand of the cultural super-ego does not trouble itself enough about the facts of the mental constitution of human beings.' Fresh tears flowed down her cheeks again.

One of her colleagues had once ventured to discuss the subject of loneliness and depression. 'Man feels lonely and sad,' he had said, 'when he wiles away his time doing nothing. There are so many things to do in the world. Feeling lonely and getting depressed are two silly things indulged by a person who is really foolish and aimless.

Man must cultivate a hobby to keep himself busy. An idle mind is a devil's workshop,' he had remarked.

A guy who knew an English proverb, idly lectured about feelings he would never understand. That was her conjecture. She had not argued. She knew he would never look at things her way.

Perhaps he belonged to the fortunate few, she reflected, clasping the warm coffee cup in her hands. The fortunate few who would never understand the two inexpressible feelings. That guy had no idea that a person suffering from loneliness or sadness would have a restless sleep. Who would understand the sleeplessness and restlessness of a depressed person, filled with anguish? An idle mind? In fact, the mind of a lonely, depressed person would be a seething volcano buried behind a made-up face presentable to society. A sunken spirit, defeated life, a sense of worthlessness, pain, insult, humiliation—a combination of all negative feelings would be assailing the poor soul to the point that it becomes impossible to focus on any other thing and other things would not be of concern to the suffering person. His or her sole concern would be to find ways and means to resolve perplexing issues! Aren't dreams and desires, depression and loneliness individualistic, subjective . . .? Maybe a supersensitive person interested in psychology and open to feelings would understand the different layers of all the painful issues that man undergoes.

She stared blankly into the dregs of the coffee mug for a while, stood up, stretched herself, heaved a deep sigh and listened to the silence of the deep night for a while. She turned and looked out the window smilingly, as a waft of cool breeze blew back her hair. Inhaling deeply, she blew a heartfelt kiss to the moonlit sky and joyed in the tranquillity it brought upon her.

With her head bent down, she trudged upstairs in the faint light of the corner night lamp, went into her daughter's room, and watched her child fast asleep. There was a corner night lamp in the kid's room, too. She pulled up the comforter to cover the girl's bare arms and closed the open window. With deep love, she bent and flicked a light kiss on her daughter's brow before she climbed down to curl up in her own bed. Before long, Neema was seeing a strange dream which made her wipe her sweaty brow unconsciously in her sleep.

She was reeling in the cold, dark, empty kitchen, prodding against the black marble counter like a drunken Maenad. A thin pencil of pale moonlight slanted on the floor from a chink in the window. Her drowsy, strained eyes were blood red, groping crazily in the dark, trying to find a way out. Her outstretched hands beat into the void and felt the invisible, cold walls. The glassy floor beneath her bare feet was chill and had little pools of black water. The hem of her nightgown was becoming wet. All she could see was a square wooden table at right angle to the black counter, with a couple of steel forks and knives that dully glinted in the faint streak of the moonlight. She grabbed a serrated knife and dashed forward in the dark.

CHAPTER NINE

She opened her eyes to a bright Sunday morning. Fortunately, she wouldn't have to see those hateful faces in her college. Still lying on the bed, she stared blankly out the window An outing for herself and Goldie was absolutely necessary. The kid needed something exciting to tell her friends at school. Her mansion was so silent and empty. Sitting on the edge of her bed, Neema pursed her lips and wondered how best she could entertain her sweet daughter.

She waddled to the kitchen for her morning cup of coffee and seated herself at the mahogany dining table in the large hall. Sipping her favourite coffee, she shot glances at the marble stairway, trying to deduce the presence of Arjun in his room from the subtle sounds that could be heard.

Probably getting ready! She heard the click of his cupboard. A thought suddenly struck her. She wanted Goldie to have a ride in her dad's car. It had been more than a year. She climbed up, and knocked on Arjun's door, rather timidly.

As soon as he opened it, she asked point blank, 'Can you drop us off to Lalbagh? That's me and Goldie in your car? She wants a drive with you.'

She watched him turn back and return to his cupboard. She repeated the question, louder and firmer standing at the entrance of the doorway. The back of his head with the arc of hair below his balding noggin shook in the negative.

'Why, what's wrong with your car?' he asked sternly without turning towards her. 'I've to meet a friend today. So I wouldn't be able to,' he said gravely.

She returned to the dining table. It was her intention to give her precious daughter a few precious moments with her father. But it was all in vain. Within minutes, he was clambering down, seemingly absorbed in his own thoughts. Instantly, she wore a smile on her mouth and turned her eyes towards the newspaper that she had spread in front of her. She sat thus until he walked past her to the foyer and put on his shoes. Within moments, she heard the main door slam. He had left. She was all alone again. Goldie was still asleep upstairs. She dully strolled to the kitchen and mixed herself another steaming cup of strong coffee.

She came out and stood with her hand on the back of the solid wood dining chair. It was a rich-looking, designer dining table. He had not spent a pie on it. The dirty bastard! She half-smiled to herself. What did he do with all his earnings? She wondered.

Finally, she straightened up, climbed upstairs to Goldie's embellished bedroom, drew open the white translucent lace curtains, and perched herself on the window sill with her cup of coffee. In the distant field, a young turbaned cowherd had squat on the crest of a low, grassy hill and was idly watching his cows graze. A sudden ennui fell on her like a dark mantle. Tears rolled down and a deep sense of loneliness closed in on her. Goldie woke up and came to her mama. With an audible yawn, she stood and watched, too, the cows grazing.

Neema smiled and stroked her head with deep affection, trying to cover up a wave of pity for the child, that was surging deep inside her.

'Where is Papa?' Goldie yawned and asked.

Neema answered that Papa was too busy with his work but had given them permission to go to Lal Bagh, so that Goldie could participate in the children's painting competition. She noticed Goldie's excitement. Neema was bombarded with questions. They quickly busied themselves with getting dressed. Goldie prattled on till they reached their destination. She wanted to know what colours to use, with whom she would sit, whether she could use red for face and blue for grass, whether she was permitted to experiment with colours . . .

The glow on her girl's face when the kid sat and ate toast and candy with other children before they started the competition was all that Neema could ask for. All smiles, Neema settled on a stone bench under a huge tree to watch her daughter do the painting.

She least imagined that Arjun could be sipping lemonade with her mother in Rajajinagar.

CHAPTER TEN

'Only the lemonade. No biscuits,' Arjun said disinterestedly. 'I'm starving, er . . . if you have cooked something.' He paused. 'Your husband has gone off on a pilgrimage. You, probably, wouldn't have cooked anything.' He looked up at Kanthi. The impatient note of angst did not go unnoticed, as he pretended to rise from the dining chair by shifting his position.

'Don't worry,' she said and busied herself in the kitchen. Within minutes, they were eating. He told her, unremittingly, what bothered him.

'What am I supposed to do now?' he thumped his fist on the wooden dining table with agony. Priya had threatened to leave him if he wouldn't marry her in the next few days. Her tears and protests had been too much for Arjun the previous evening. He had telephoned Kanthi and the latter had suggested that he meet her, as her husband wouldn't be at home. Priya had threatened to go to the police and the press to report that he had cheated not only his wife, but her, too. And she had raved at him with tears streaming down her eyes. Arjun couldn't lose her.

Losing her would mean losing the dream of becoming the landlord he had dreamt of.

Kanthi listened, deeply reflecting on what he had said. 'We'll soon do something about this. Don't worry.' She pursed her lips in deep thought. Eventually, a sly smile crossed her face.

She went to the kitchen, brought two mugs of coffee, seated herself, and said calmly, 'Take your family on a picnic soon. Some hill station, perhaps, where there are waterfalls.'

She saw him sit upright and drop his jaw in utter amazement.

'Well, do as I say now,' she said firmly with a smile. 'It is easy to get her out of the way, if you take them on a picnic.' She noticed his perplexed face. 'You can send Goldie to a residential school. She is a big girl now,' she said placidly in a cold tone, paused and looked at the floor, as if reflecting upon something.

'I want you to do me a favour in return,' she said and disappeared into the room. She came back with a file containing some documents and sat on the couch. 'Before my father-in-law died, he made a will bequeathing his property to his two sons, the younger being my husband.' She looked down at the documents, holding them firmly in her hand, and continued, 'He left the papers with the family attorney, a close and trusted friend of his who lived in Mysore. This man made a telephone call a few years ago, asked for my husband, and since my husband was not at home at that time, he spoke to me. He requested me to meet him at the earliest, as he was dying of terminal cancer. He said that he had some important documents, papers given to him by my father-in-law before his death. My husband didn't show much interest, so I was compelled to make the trip alone and get the papers. According to the will, my father-in-law has left behind gold and silver worth a crore, besides a bungalow on the outskirts of Mysore that approximates to about twelve crore. He also has a few bonds worth some lakhs. My husband's elder brother lives comfortably and luxuriously in a village and is not on speaking terms with us and till now hasn't shown any interest in his father's property. He has a son who is a scientist. He is married and living happily in the United States of America, and I don't think he will ever challenge the will. So please go ahead and prepare a will making me the beneficiary of all the assets mentioned in this will.'

Arjun scratched his forehead with the back of his right thumb, completely perplexed. He took the papers. 'It's rather difficult,' he said, speculating upon the burdensome responsibility. 'Both you and I maybe at risk in the future.'

'You will help me in this matter, won't you?' she asked sceptically. 'You are a legal expert and I bet you can do this with ease.' She pulled out a blank sheet from the file. Holding it up she said, 'here is a blank sheet with my husband's finger print on it. Perhaps, this would come of use to you.' She smiled unabatedly.

'Can I expect a fee for this?' He grinned sheepishly.

'I have just given you a wonderful suggestion. Haven't I?' She walked up to him and patted him on the shoulder. 'That's going to open up opportunities for you, right?'

He got up, strolled to the armchair in the hall, sat at ease, and finally looked relaxed when he took in a deep breath. Kanthi settled on the couch opposite him with a smirk.

'You have been a strong and courageous person, my dear son-in-law. Tell me one thing,' she said. 'How come you are impassive towards your daughter, too?'

'Haven't you done the same thing?' he guffawed. 'It's I who pay my daughter's educational fees. I keep money on the dining table every morning for her other expenditures. Sometimes more, sometimes less which she can spend in whatever way she wants to. The rest, I ignore.' He shrugged in annoyance.

'You lied about one thing at the time of marriage,' he said after a pause, 'You told me that your daughter would soon walk out if neglected. That she was headstrong, proud, and independent.'

'She is! But I don't know what has held her back. Atleast, her pride is broken,' Kanthi simpered.

'I must thank my friend Shravana for teaching me how to ignore your daughter and deny her the rightful place as a wife. That's what you expected of me. Didn't you? To crush your daughter's proud spirit by withholding all that a husband should give his lawful wife. Not sleeping with her as a husband or even touching her is enough to kill the heart and soul of a wife, but your daughter seems to be a tough person,' he said with a sneer.

Kanthi disappeared into the kitchen and brought some more coffee. 'That tough person must be knocked off now,' she said resolutely.

'I don't want her to be part of the wealth that I may acquire. She has been rebellious and haughty always."

Finally he stood, twisted his waist in both directions to limber himself up, yawned widely, and left with the will.

CHAPTER ELEVEN

After Arjun left, Kanthi sat gloomily on the sofa with anger and regret. Arjun had accused her of cheating him. A few years after her daughter's marriage, she had disclosed the fact that she hated her daughter and had earnestly believed that Arjun's indifference would throw her out on the streets. But Neema walked about with her spirits up. She and Goldie were doing so well and getting along so well. Arjun was disgusted and so was she. He couldn't marry Priya without a divorce.

With anger mounting in her, Kanthi attributed all this to the adoration her husband had for Neema. It was his undue, overt love for the girl that had made her so confident. He had always liked Neema more than Mili.

Her mind journeyed to the past when she herself was younger. He would pounce on her from corners and make love, play pachisi game every weekend. He took her out for movies and hotels to eat masala dosa, but after the birth of the first girl, Neema, his love got divided. She didn't tolerate it. She would become furious when she would see him hug his girl and play the clown to make her laugh.

'Look at her dimples!' he would coo, carrying the girl all over the house, smack kisses with such fondness and got so engaged in playing with his little daughter that Kanthi's rage went unheeded. Thus in the course of time, her rage had turned to jealousy and her jealousy to hatred.

She observed that as Neema grew up, she had begun to draw the attention of the public and of all relatives and friends who visited them. Her sweet voice, spirited talk, and charming look left people praising her, and Kanthi sharply felt that Mili was side-lined.

'Neema is adorable,' they said, 'Easy-going, warm-hearted, very friendly, and . . .' Neema's dimpled, charming smile always became another topic of their brief discussion. As the two girls grew up, what Kanthi could not stand anymore was people's overt praise for Neema with only a bare smile to Mili, and she, in turn, would not bother to smile at them. People always complimented Neema for one thing or the other and Mili would just go unnoticed.

Kanthi could not endure it. Mili, her second daughter, would be hanging around, clinging to her sari. People hardly paid any attention to her. They spoke to Neema alone in a more engaging manner. Neema loved to prattle and was capable of making others laugh, whereas Mili was sober and hovered around her mother, looking at people in disdain. Neema experimented with styles and makeovers and was quick to catch up with the changing trends. And Kanthi loathed her all the more. Whereas Mili submissively gave in to her mama's wishes and went about her life in a sheepish way. Whenever Neema tied a high ponytail, Kanthi would pull off the band, or when she put her two plaits over her shoulders to the front, Kanthi would simply tug them back and fling curses at her. In spite of all this, Neema had one day been daring enough to cut the ends and curl some hair on her brow.

She wore slippers to the dining room, ate ice in winter, and got up only after seven in the mornings without setting up alarm, inspite of her mother's accusations.

'Rebellious! Always rebellious,' Kanthi would scream with venom in her tone and would complain to her husband, but he would simply pass it off, saying, 'She is young. Forgive her.'

Ah! The girl always thought that she was too smart. People's appreciation and admiration had further added fuel to Kanthi's growing fire of jealousy and envy. In fact, she had begun to neglect Neema much earlier, when she was just a child.

'Your dad will come and wait on you,' she would say when Neema was just in school, and go about her household chores.

What began as indifference had slowly turned to dislike, and dislike had metamorphosed to hatred as Neema bloomed into a young woman.

Her hatred for Neema, eventually, had vitrified into a venomous insouciance. In fact, it had congealed beyond thinning. Her fury had shot up all the more when her husband had once suggested, 'You must get some psychological treatment.'

Neema did not belong to her as a daughter anymore. Kanthi's unwarranted resolution to destroy the girl's very psyche, her intangible pride, as she perceived it, solidified into a mission she chased in a grotesque manner that put her in the place of a stepmother. She hated Neema with all her heart and her ultimate resolution was that Neema must sink in emotional disorder.

CHAPTER TWELVE

It was the fag end of July and Neema had started decorating the house with gusto. Goldie's birthday had always been one occasion that pepped up her spirits and gave her an opportunity to throw a party at home. Goldie had invited her whole class for her birthday party. What's more, her grandpa had arrived early to have breakfast with them and had brought gifts and gems. Grandma had said that she would join in the afternoon with other relatives.

Grandma arrived late afternoon, bringing her sister and sister-in-law. Although both aunts secretly knew about Neema's marital discord, Kanthi's sister questioned peremptorily, while helping Neema with the preparation of salad, 'Any news of a second baby, Neema?' She was shrewd enough to cap off her cynical question with a good, hearty laugh.

Neema poured the boiling water over the coffee powder and turned towards her. 'He has not slept with me for years,' she quibbled and gulped down the instant sadness that the question had brought on her. 'Not that you don't know about it,' she added.

'Common, he looks a sexy guy and . . .' continued her aunty.

'This girl is short-tempered. She puts him off. How will he ever like her?' her mother butted in.

Neema's blood began to boil. 'Why do you want to pass wrong comments?' She queried and stared at her mother angrily.

'Didn't I say she is short-tempered?' Kanthi glanced at the ladies triumphantly as if substantiating her point. Her sister-in-law, who was two years older than her, who hadn't intervened yet was laughing, treating it all as a joke. Her mom removed the fruits from the refrigerator and turned to her sister.

'What's the big deal if her husband doesn't sleep with her?' she said, arranging the fruits in a tray. 'This is a lustful girl! He is a marvellous husband—he polishes the kid's shoes, irons her uniform, puts clothes into the washing machine, and even cooks occasionally when this girl is out on her duty. What more do you want?' she exchanged glances with them.

'It is not just sex, Ma.' Neema threw her gaze at her mother. 'He doesn't even talk to me. Till today, he has not bought me a gift. He doesn't even sit with me on the same sofa. He is not a husband in any manner.'

Kanthi gulped down a wave of pleasure.

Her sister looked up towards Neema, 'What your mom says is right, Neema,' she said in support of Kanthi's words,

'Sex is not all that important. Thank God! Your husband doesn't physically or mentally ill treat you. And as per your mom's verdict, he seems to be a perfect husband. He is a busy lawyer. Don't forget that.'

Neema forced a pale, tight smile on her face and busied herself with tidying up the kitchen. However, the forces of revolt whirled within her. She was prompted to speak out another chunk of her thought later. She let the thought frame into a meaningful sentence and took her own time in wording it.

While serving them coffee upstairs in the balcony, she questioned her aunts, 'Do you know that sex is an essential part of married life to strengthen marital bond?'

Her aunts started laughing with cups shaking in their hands. 'We didn't know,' they said almost in unison.

Although Neema realised instantly that she had made herself the butt of their ridicule, she felt relieved that at least she had not kept quiet like a dumb person. 'Many divorces actually take place because of sexual dissatisfaction,' she avouched. The women stopped laughing and nodded their heads.

'Then what are you waiting for?' Kanthi's sister asked slyly, winking at her sister.

Neema gulped down the sarcasm with a smile. Her dad showed up upstairs. 'What's going on?' he asked cheerfully.

Neema left them and climbed downstairs, blinking her eyes several times to clear the gathering tears.

Goldie turned thirteen with élan, least knowing that the pleasure of going to her grandparents' house would come to an end that year, for on the night of Diwali, three months later, her grandpa passed away in his sleep.

CHAPTER THIRTEEN

Neema had a lot to share with her friend Pada. She headed towards her friend's staff room down the breezy corridor. Giggles and voices of some ladies sailed through the half open door. Before she could push the door open, she heard her name being mentioned by them. She stood still. She was not an eavesdropper, but a certain degree of anxiety and curiosity arrested her movement.

A gutsy voice cried out amidst loud laughter, 'Neema is crazy to flirt with Milan, a guy who turns up after several years.'

So Pada had told them all whatever she had shared with her? Extra colours were being added to their gossip. Neema took a deep breath and froze at the threshold.

'God knows why she quarrels with her husband and blames him for not sleeping with her,' said another calm voice in a detached manner.

'He doesn't even talk to her,' conjoined Pada in high-pitched intensity.

'That's because she doesn't deserve it,' said another singsong voice with a hearty giggle.

'You are right,' declared a more familiar voice. 'The other day, I shaid to her to shatishfy hish shtomach to win hish love. She didn't even hear it. She walked away in anger. I don't think she cooks tashty thingsh for him.'

There was laughter and giggles. The first voice said loudly, 'She is too bold. Look at the way she comes stylishly dressed in spite of being punished by God. You must hear the way she argues about women's liberation and man's chauvinism. Oh, my God! Any man will be put off by her arguments. She is a very daring character. How can her husband like her?'

'We better close this topic. She may drop by any time,' said Pada, and there were sounds of chairs and the rustle of saris.

Neema turned back and retraced her steps in haste, but she didn't go to her staff room. She lumbered to the canteen. There were tears flooding in her chest and her heart was palpitating faster.

Months ago, Pada had encouraged her to take Milan as her boyfriend. 'Why don't you accept Milan as your boyfriend? There's nothing wrong in that,' she had said.

Sipping coffee mindlessly at the wooden table in the canteen, Neema recalled those false words of her friend. Those friendly, encouraging words were a farce. She finally got up and marched to her staff room.

For the first time, it dawned on Neema that friendship had no value in a metropolitan city. People laughed if you cried and cried if you laughed. Sitting alone in her staff room minutes later, she recalled Tom Hanks and his words as told to the little boy in his film, *The Polar Express*: 'Friendship is the greatest gift of life.' She had watched and enjoyed the movie with Goldie on a Sunday afternoon on Star Movies from the comfort of her living room, with pakoras and coffee.

That was only a computer animated fantasy film, she told herself and took in a deep breath and brightened up her face with difficulty before she prepared to leave for the day.

A dismal hint of a smile curled on her lips under her vapid eyes. After much pondering, her one resolution was to get some tranquilising pills on her way home.

She turned the key in her car after her last class at four o'clock and started to drive. The sun was scorching hot. She cranked up the windows, put on her goggles, and drove mechanically, looking at the world through her tear-filled eyes. The roads and route were all so familiar. A heavy ennui hung on her and a sensation of emptiness lay heavily in the pit of her stomach. An inexpressible emotional pain, a sense of loss, a kind of dizziness, numbness in her head, and a feeling of loneliness blindfolded her. She knew she needed help from someone she could trust. *A counsellor?* They only listened. She wanted some soothing words of love from some affectionate, warm-hearted person who could convince her, comfort her, and empathise with her torn self, someone who would understand her confused state of mind. There was none she could think of. The only option she could think of was to go home straight and plunk on her bed under a sheet. She didn't want to see the world. The glaring, naked truth of deceit and hypocrisy, pretence and slyness masked shamelessly in the name of friendship . . . she was furious with the world. Her right hand steered while her left was on the gear.

For most of her married life, she had slept alone, longing to be in the arms of a man. She had even pushed aside her love feelings for Milan and had suppressed her longing to accept him as her boyfriend. After her marriage, there were but a few nights when she had not wept in her bed in an effort to take life in stride. Yet people spoke about her, laughed at her misfortune. Had she not tried to be the good wife? She had served Arjun's parents like a dog, because respecting elders was in her blood. Hadn't she learnt new dishes solely to please him? He had been indifferent to everything.

With tears blinding her eyes, she brought her car to a screeching halt. A teenager on a cycle sped in front of her moving car with a smart, daring smile. She drove on. She saw a medical store to her left. Would the pharmacist give her some anti-depressant pills or sleeping pills? She doubted it. She didn't know any particular name of any brand. She drove on. She veered on a never-ending macadamised road. She had taken a wrong turn. She took another U-turn onto a cobbled street and reached home battling with angst, rage, and tears that threatened to knock out from her puffed-up, rufescent face. She fumbled in her purse for the key. Everything seemed dark. Dazed and benumbed, she turned the key in the hole and shut the door behind her.

She lay listless in the darkness of the falling twilight for a long time. The noon sun had descended and the blazing heat had dropped by degrees. Her beautiful, fish-like eyes, shelved into little weeping islands, hardly batted as she slouched and stared dumbly outside through her bedroom window. She had been foolish in listening credulously to the words of some elders who had convinced her that the birth of a child would resolve her relationship with Arjun. She had eagerly begot a baby. The fact that Arjun's indifference towards her was intentional had gripped her thoughts very late. Their lives had fallen apart.

He had put his hand around her bare waist and had made love to her on that chilly night of twenty-third December, almost a year after their marriage, though he never slept with her ever again after impregnating her. She had enjoyed every moment of her new and wonderful experience of pregnancy and confinement. The new born had kept her busy and she had revelled in the joy of having become a mother. Arjun had distanced himself from her further, showing no signs of affection or joy for his baby, either. Was the pregnancy by accident? She wondered now. He had not even hugged her after that.

She had spent many nights dozing off on the couch in the living room, anticipating his return with dishes cooling off on the dining table, hoping to turn him on, but he always came home heavily drunk and avouched that he was tired with a mouth that bore the repulsive smell of liquor and garlic and would belch right in her face.

A draught of cold air blew from her bedroom window as she lay still on the bed ruminating over a myriad thought.

She finally stirred and pulled herself up. Minutes later, she plodded to the kitchen, made herself a cup of steaming coffee, and shuffled to the living room.

She drew open the white translucent lace curtains of the bay window. It was dark outside. A tiny sob erupted from her throat. She let a pale, whimsical smile creep up her parched lips to subdue her erupting sobs. The lines of Rupert Brooke ran in her mind:

The pain, the calm, and the astonishment,

Desire illimitable and still content,

And all dear names men use, to cheat despair,

For the perplexed and viewless streams that bear

Our hearts at random down the dark of life,

Now, ere the unthinking silence on that strife

Steals down, I would cheat drowsy Death so far.

She carried another cup of coffee and sat herself on the couch, staring out into the breezy darkness. She realised Goldie had crept into her bed. She was in the eighth grade and had grown into a responsible young lady.

The next morning after Goldie and Arjun had left, Neema picked up the remote and switched on the television. She pressed the buttons on the remote lackadaisically. However, her mind cogitated on a number of other things.

She had no friends with whom she could unburden the heaviness of her heart. She didnot have anybody to call her own except for Goldie, who now tended to live in her own world. Sadness crept into her eyes. She let her tears flow freely. When her eyes were drained, she felt hungry but couldnot be more concerned about it than her present situation. The tune of a wedding band could be faintly heard in the distance.

There was no one to telephone her or cheer her up or pull her out of her blue. Melancholia and loneliness sat heavy on her bosom like a metallic garrotte. She didnot bother to get dressed or attend her college. She didnot go out the next day, or the next. Three days passed by. She had developed apathy for her workplace. Her tears mutely gurgled within her like a tiny surging ocean, lapping the walls of her cells. She was too tired to let it out. Her swollen, red eyes had become almost dry. She didn't bother to go back to work. Goldie was busy with her own self. Like her dad, she would leave silently while Neema would still be in bed.

In a way, Neema became less concerned about her daughter. Sitting for hours on the sofa in the quiet living room, she watched in the air the spectre of events through which she had sailed in her life like a decrepit woman lost and worn out; tired and blank in a meaningless world with the sting of sadness in her beautiful eyes.

The cool, dark, tranquil hours of the night became the crib of Neema's reminiscence. She sat hour after hour through the darkness of the nights at the oval-shaped, black granite counter in the kitchen and soliloquised in whispers. The moon and the stars became her sole, loving companions.

Chapter Fourteen

Arjun shared with Shravana what Kanthi had suggested. They discussed other options to execute the operation of exterminating Neema. A few days later, Arjun informed Kanthi what Shravana proposed and got her approval for it.

Almost a month passed by before Shravana could procure the poisonous powder. He put it in a little pouch and gave it to Arjun, who was tensely going over the plan day in and day out.

Once he had the drug, he decided to hatch the picnic topic with Neema. It had to be in the morning. He carefully went through the stratagem he had resolved to adopt. Going downstairs early in the morning under the pretext of removing his car from the garage would flex up things with her, he hoped. He conjectured that the tense atmosphere that prevailed between them could be eased out. He was confident that he could get her to talk to him by a flick of his magnanimous act.

He fidgeted about in his room in the early hours of the morning and rehearsed the words that he would utter and the expression he would wear on his visage. He picked up his car key and walked down the stairs. Neema was there at the dining table, sipping coffee with the newspaper in front of her. As soon as she sensed him climbing down, she bent over the page with a spruced-up countenance and, with a seeming touch of pleasure, dragged a sip of the hot beverage and with an affected gravity began running her eyes over the news lines, while he bent his head with pretended contemplation and walked past her.

After having put his car outside the garage, he ambled to the dining table and stood with a fake guilty expression, toggling with his car key.

'After our last trip to Ooty many years ago, we haven't gone out anywhere,' he said slowly and calculatedly. His gaze was fixed on the key he was fumbling with in his palm.

Forgotten memories came flooding into Neema's mind. Three months after their marriage, her dad had pressured Arjun to take her on a honeymoon. Years ago, when they had made their first trip, she was quite excited to begin her life's long, unknown journey. But nothing exciting had happened.

'I have been thinking . . .' He finally looked at her. Marble-like green orbs moved in his vacant, moist eyes. 'I've been thinking that we should go on a picnic this weekend,' he said with a fake beseeching expression.

She gave a little smile.

Why was he saying that? What plans? Was he trying to change to a better person? Had Goldie's angel blessed the kid finally by giving her the opportunity to spend some time with her dad?

Thoughts bordering on scepticism raced through her mind. She stood up with the coffee cup in her hand, and turned to go to the kitchen. He followed her and stood in the doorway. She caught his expressionless, brooding face as she turned to rinse the cup.

'You didn't give me an answer. Let's go to Yercaud this time,' he said.

'Sure, we will go,' she replied.

In the evening, after Goldie returned from school, Neema broke the news to her with much fervour and excitement. There were tears in her eyes when she saw the bloom on the girl's face. The girl was soon telephoning her friends to say that she was going on a picnic with both her parents.

Goldie followed her dad as he busied himself dumping all the packed stuff into the boot. She had a number of questions, but the only answers she got from him were, *Just wait and see or . . . Hmm* or a stern *One second.* She wanted to help him put the luggage into the car, but he didnot want her help.

It was Neema who kept her occupied throughout the journey by feeding her inquisitiveness. They played word games and hummed Bollywood songs. Neema also had interesting stories of classical literature to narrate tirelessly.

It was breakfast time, about a quarter to ten, when they reached Yercaud, the beautiful hill station of Salem district in Tamil Nadu known for its citrus fruits, especially oranges.

Arjun finally pulled the car in front of a pretty cottage that featured an excellent view of the surrounding misty, lush green Shevaroy Hills. The property had been booked by his close friend, Shravana, who as a civil engineer had good contacts.

A watchman in a tuxedo and a green woollen cap hurried down the four steps, brought his palms together, and greeted them with a 'namasthe' and said humbly that he had been looking forward to their arrival.

The mild, soft rays of a damp August afternoon sun slanted onto the porch of their accommodation, giving some warmth for Neema to stand in the natural spotlight, looking at the picturesque surroundings.

Arjun's thick, wide, slimy mouth drew into a fictitious smile in an effort to mask the consternation that he was going through. He followed the watchman with his hands in his pockets.

How the hell did Kanthi think that he could do it? It wasn't so easy. He checked his shirt pocket. The tiny packet with the poison powder was absolutely safe. *Shravana had arranged for it and Kanthi had approved of it. If giving her the powder unobtrusively is not possible, walk her to the edge of the cliff on the top, show her the plunging waterfall, and your work is done with a slight push. I need not explain further. Not a difficult task. Nobody will suspect you,* Kanthi had assured him.

Her words reverberated in his mind. He stood on the chilly porch and watched his wife and daughter playing on the expanse of grass that had a wonderful rim of rose bushes well maintained by the cottage management. In her excitement, Goldie had climbed over the three-foot-tall mortared stone wall, its façade covered with bushes, fascinated by the plunging valleys and the tiny wild flowers that jutted out from the narrow spaces of the wall. Neema gazed, wonder struck, at the little misty town that lay in the valley down below with their little red tile tops, singular tiny houses halfway up the forested hills, shrouded in mystery and shrubs. However, her grip on Goldie's wrist didnot lose her attention.

'If you can hurry up, please,' Arjun called out to them, 'we can have breakfast and go trekking,' he said. Neema and Goldie rushed into the room and got freshened up in no time. The watchman brought breakfast to the porch, but they sat inside the warmth of the cosy cottage on the pillowed cane chairs, for Goldie said she felt cold outside.

In about an hour, they were climbing the summit. He was in the front, ten metres away, leading them.

Goldie was holding her mama's fingers tightly. The steep climb up the crag with pebbles and brush was rather trying. Mother and daughter halted occasionally to pick up a pebble or admire the waterfall cascading to the rocky chasm. As they trekked, Neema tripped once over a boulder and fell on her bums. Goldie screamed and grabbed her mama's dress. Arjun stopped and turned around. He saw Neema scrambling to her feet. He abruptly turned back and was walking away again, musing over the unwanted uphill trek which was, he felt, nothing but an undesirable, deliberate task. Goldie called out, asking him to wait, but his pretended deafness took the better of him and he walked on.

Neema let out a small giggle and convinced her daughter that she was fine. They sat and leisured. Neema brought out a packet of biscuits and Nestlé chocolate from her small, green backpack. They turned their heads and swept their vision up about hundred metres away, where Arjun was standing with an arm akimbo and holding on to the trunk of a tree with his other hand.

After a few minutes, the pair was up on their feet again. When they got close, Arjun started to move off. The magnificent view of the Shevaroy hill range and the smoking mist on their shady summits and the descending vaporous chilly sky was unimaginably breath taking. They were about three hundred feet up on the hill from the confluence of water from the Yercaud Lake and other reaches that cascaded gloriously onto the folds of the rocky wall and fell ferociously into the Kiliyur valley. 'Isn't this enchanting, Goldie?' Neema asked, holding her hand. Goldie nodded her head in approval, looking ahead. She then threw a glance at Arjun. With arms akimbo, he was watching the chasm at the bottom, where fine spray was being splashed monstrously in all its splendour. *Goldie can be sent to a residential school*, Kanthi had said. The words echoed and re-echoed in his restless brain. He suddenly turned to them and said, looking at Goldie, 'These are the eastern ghats of Tamil Nadu. Isn't it beautiful?' The girl nodded and stood watching the surroundings with crossed hands.

When they had reached the summit, he walked up to them and took Neema's hand, much to her pleasure and surprise, imploringly instructed Goldie to stay back for a few minutes, and led Neema forward almost to the edge where the roaring gush of water was taking its plunge. 'Isn't beautiful, Neema?' he asked, turning his head to her side. Overcome with emotion for umpteen reasons, Neema managed to nod in silence with a little smile which he didnot even care to notice. His heart was drumming inside as he laid his hand on her shoulder with his practised pseudo-smile of friendship. While they stood with their feet in the shallow, flowing stream, he scrupulously scanned the surroundings for the last time.

Three hundred feet below in the distance, standing at the outer edge of the pool formed by the waterfall was a young couple looking up at the point fromwhere the water cascaded. He didn't care for them much. *They couldn't be looking at us.* He concluded. A small group of young men were under the cascading falls, screaming and bathing under the natural 'Jacuzzi', a word which they were screaming. It rose in the air and faintly reached the ears of those who were up at the summit. Arjun observed that they were at their own game. He purportedly stepped on a tiny pebble and in a dramatic infirmity quickly gripped Neema's shoulder as pre-planned. Her right foot skid, glided a foot in one go. Her waist had plunged forward when she took control of herself and grabbed Arjun's arm in consternation with a rictal mouth and terror-stricken eyes. He tried to pull his shirt off, but her grip was tighter than he had expected and he too, slipped involuntarily, his heart racing wildly. He held her wrist for support, for she had taken a stance with her feet firmly pressed against a boulder, and they came to a halt just a few steps away from the plunge. He shook his head in disgust, turned, and started to walk away. The young couple below was screaming, 'Take care, buddy.'

Neema slowly and carefully pulled off her sandals and followed suit on her bare feet for a better grip on the pebbled stream. She walked nervously, with apprehension and disquietude surmounting her for having made this trip with the man who had never been a husband, had never slept with her after Goldie's birth, nor had ever hugged her nor exhibited any kind of love, even by words, nor had ever made a good, loving father, either. In no time, they were on their way back to the cottage.

They ate in a restaurant in silence and went for a nap once back in their accommodation. She and Goldie rolled on the double bed, while Arjun threw himself on the single one with a nightstand separating the two cots.

It was late evening, dark and chill, when they woke up. After sipping coffee, Neema and Goldie started to play 'catch me if you can' on the grass while Arjun sat in the porch affectedly reading a novel and intermittently chatting with the watchman who waited on him with servitude.

'From where can you get us food?' Arjun finally asked.

'There is a small hotel, sir, a few kilometres away. Run by a couple. They prepare delicious food within no time.'

The watchman sounded very assuring. Arjun listened without lifting up his eyes. He ran his right index finger over his thick, clammy, chapped lower lip while his ruffled eyebrows were arched upin deep contemplation, making a myriad creases on his white forehead. With his forefoot on the ground, he was wildly shaking his left leg, as if pounding something.

'Anything the matter, sir?' enquired the watchman with concern.

Arjun lifted up his face towards him and asked almost impatiently, 'Can you get me chilled beer from somewhere?' He kept stroking his thick lower lip with his thumb.

'Beer, sir?' The watchman's voice sounded a bit hesitant. Standing in the shadow, beyond the dimly glowing single neon bulb that oscillated from a length of wire above the cane furniture, the watchman asked 'How many bottles, sir?' Trying to stifle a yawn in the wind.

'We are celebrating, Neema,' Arjun called out. 'I'm ordering for beer. You will drink with me a little tonight, won't you?' he queried. His thick, broad, slimy lips repulsively became wider with his artificial smile. She merely smiled and waved 'What shall I order for Goldie?' he called out. The girl heard him and screamed out, 'A Coke,' and that was added to the list of finger snacks and beer.

The watchman left and in less than an hour was meticulously laying the bottles and glasses on the glass-topped round rattan teapoy inside the cottage on Arjun's instruction. Salted peanuts, butter chips, and pakoras were poured into the large tray in three tiny heaps. The peon handed over the bottle of Coke to the girl with a smile and went out. He climbed his cycle again to get them hot food from the nearby restaurant.

For the first time, Arjun sat across Neema and looked into her eyes.

His green orbs in his moist eyes gazed at her as he mentally ran over the thing he had to do now.

'You look tired,' she said quietly.

He straightened himself in the chair and smiled. He opened the ice container, and popped open two bottles of beer, exhilarated within, with the fact that she would now drink the stuff without an iota of suspicion.

Rubbing the tip of his nose with the back of his index finger, he reflected upon the fact that she who disliked even the smell of beer and had puked in the first year of their marriage, when he had come home heavily drunk, exhaling its strong smell, had conceded to drink tonight with him. He checked his pocket again to make sure that it still held the little packet.

Neema, who kept watching him, took a deep breath to allay the sudden emotion of pity that had risen in her. She noted his pathetic countenance. Like he really meant to say, *Will you forgive me, please?*

She experienced a wave of unremitting love overriding her. *If only he had opened out his arms, she would run into him and cuddle his tired-looking face like she would do to a child.*

A myriad thought crossed Neema's mind as she sat and relaxed and wondered how best she could make use of the opportunity that God had sent her to repair their devastated relationship.

Their marriage anniversary was fast approaching and was he making amends to set right their relationship? Was it not her duty to grab this moment to bring some changes in his thinking? Maybe she had unnecessarily misconstrued the morning incident.

'You would want to rinse the glasses, wouldn't you?' He asked.

'Oh, yeah,' she said and picked up the glasses. As she strolled to the washbasin with a teeny pleasure catching up on her, she caught his face in the mirror above the sink in those few paces. A chill ran down her spine suddenly. He was staring at her back like a murderer, fumbling for something in his shirt pocket. There was cruelty in the glint of his eyes; he had sucked the corners of his mouth in his icy stare. There was villainy and evilness in his visage. To keep her racing heart under check, she turned back quickly and called out, 'Goldie.'

The girl, who was playing with the watchman's little girl in the portico, came running inside with a loud 'Yes, mama? Papa, something fell down from your pocket,' she called out, casting a brief glance at the tiny white packet that had fallen under the teapoi, as she scuttled towards her mother.

Neema walked back just when he slipped it back into his pocket. She drank with him a little with a pretended smile and lulled Goldie to sleep. It was almost twelve when the two finished their dinner. She was least interested in asking him anything.

When Neema opened her eyes in the morning, the cottage looked empty and silent, with Goldie still sleeping beside her. A slanting shaft of bright, soft sunrays filtered through the small, rectangular glass inlaid in the ceiling. She was in no mood to get up. *Did the picnic offer me anything interesting for a change? Not that I had any hopes for it.* An ironical smile caught her mouth for a brief moment. She had gone to bed in a deep panic. A drop of unchecked tear rolled down her cheek. Anyway, she told herself that she had come on this picnic mainly for Goldie's happiness.

They had a sumptuous breakfast silently and checked out before noon. He started off the drive preoccupied with his own thoughts.

Everything seemed weird to Neema as the drive continued. *Why had he brought them on this trip?* She wondered. She had hoped for an apology and a hug. Or had he expected that from her? But she had not done anything wrong, she mutely contended.

Undesirable memories rose from their slumber again, overwhelming her with remorse and humiliation and making her hate herself for continuing to live with the man who had slighted her so severely.

Her Venusian dreams of romance and fun had all been trampled to dust. What was this outing for? She couldnot figure it out. She had hoped for a relationship revival. She didn't want to think any more about it. With tears welling in her eyes, she inclined her seat and dozed off.

He, on the other hand, was overwrought with disappointment. The trip had proved disastrous and a sheer waste. Kanthi would be expecting some good news. *He couldn't carry out a small task. Ah, but of a monstrous nature! What if he had been caught as a suspect?* He pursed his lips in apprehension. He cast a sideward glance at Neema and his mind screamed in indignation—*Let her go to the devil!* He was simply unable to get rid of her. She had not walked out on him, no matter what he did. His anger mounted uncontrollably—anger not just towards her, but anger at his own self for not being able to get rid of her and anger towards Kanthi for making such a task sound so simple.

He brought his car to a screeching halt. 'I'm going to have a tender coconut. How about you?' he asked her solemnly, getting out of the car without even glancing at her. Goldie was asleep in the backseat. Neema said she would have it too and got out of the vehicle.

It was a long, silent drive. They reached home at twilight.

CHAPTER FIFTEEN

Neema was back to her routine college work.

Goldie was growing up fast and was already in her mid-teens. Neema watched her daughter blossom into a young woman with sheer joy. Whether Arjun was home or not, it didn't matter in the least. Like a grey, gloomy day when it neither rains nor shines, Neema walked about in gloom, wondering why Arjun never held her by the waist like other husbands, why even during the first few months of their marriage, he never turned around in bed and caressed her, which she had so much looked forward to. During those few months, he would come home in the afternoons for lunch, which she considered an honour to be able to cook for him, but he would neither speak nor laugh nor touch her and had thus negated the very essence of their marital relationship. Rather, he lay like the chiselled stone statue of Lord Mahaveer that she had seen with her dad as a schoolgirl, with a broad, silent smile on his mouth and eyes peacefully closed, leaving ashes in her mouth.

Her loving dad was gone forever, making her almost an orphan. Goldie never showed interest in visiting her grandma. She cursed herself for having lost touch with Milan, too. He who loved her so much! She remembered the words he had said on the day of their last meeting, when he had picked her up from her college and had taken her to airport road for icecream. 'I'm always there for you,'he had said. Now she didn't know where he was.

All that was left to her now was their apparition that came back, beckoning her to their hearts.

Mili, after her marriage a couple of years ago to a small-time businessman, who owned a garment shop of his own in the suburbs of Bangalore, had completely severed her relationship with Neema.

Neema had not walked away from Arjun because she was afraid of society's criticism. What would she answer them, those inquisitive people, if at all they asked about her husband? All her fiery talk on women's empowerment as a college girl had simply frizzled out with time and actuality. She loathed herself for not having the courage to face the flippant talk of society if she lived as a single mother. Also, she didnot want Goldie to become fatherless, either. If she had to protect Goldie from the hawk-like eyes of indecent men, her belief was that a father figure at home was the best option.

One summer night in late June, she jolted awake from her sleep. She switched on the airconditioner and let her eyes meekly wander to the solitary, monotonous night light in the corner outside her bedroom, where the white marble stairs with its rosewood banister wound upwards, ghostlike, in the quiet, dark hall. She sat in her bed in her silk nightgown, unable to sleep. She got up and strode out. The white geometrical patterns on the little brown carpet on the floor beneath the dining table looked uncanny in the dark.

Her heart was beating unreasonably hard and sweat wetted her smooth brow. She sat on the cold marble steps of her huge housethat was shrouded in semidarkness to reflect upon her life. Except for the sound of crickets outside, everything seemed to be so quiet.

*What course hasmy life taken? Where is it heading to?*She inhaled and exhaled deeply. *Even birds migrate seasonally to suit themselves. Ah!What am Idoing here?*

She brought down her hand from her temple and mused over her long, dreary existence in an opulent house in which she had become a mannequin. To survive in a society that had less regard for single women was not easy. Only those women who proved their tenacity as culture-conscious, dignified wives, no matter how they were treated by their husbands or in-laws, were held in esteem.

She climbed up the stairs slowly, looked at her daughter's pretty, innocent face, and fondly ran her fingers over the girl's head. The kid missed her granddad. She kissed her girl on the brow and climbed down again quietly.

The need for a divorce loomed large in her mind.

She stood by the wooden bookcase and picked up a Jane Austen. *Probably he would turn up in the morning.* She needed to talk to him immediately. Leaning against it, listless, she flicked a few pages, put it back, ran her fingers over the row of books and pulled out *Emma*. Nothing interested her. She needed a divorce. And that was it. She put *Emma* back in its slot and pulled out Irving Wallace. She riffled through its pages idly, and then became restless. Her eyes brimmed with tears. She pressed her lids and allowed the drops to roll down her cheeks. She put the book back and picked up a dictionary. *He has not gifted me a single item in all these years of our married life. There have been no marriage anniversaries or a party hosted ever since I married him. Tell me, God. Am I being false?* Tears were streaming down her face.

Not once had he called her darling like the way her uncles did when they spoke with their wives. Somehow, that word coming out of a lover's mouth had mesmerised her. She had longed to hear it from Arjun. She would have foregone the sex part of her marriage had he at least been communicative with her and behaved like a normal human being. If only he had been on talking terms with her! But there was nothing of anything. She pulled a tissue from the cardboard box that was on the top of the bookcase and blew her nose. *What am I doing with a dictionary?* She frowned and flipped it on top of the bookcase and waited for his return.

She strode into the dark, silent living room and switched on the television. Most of the channels were running only commercials. *Idiot box!* She switched it off with animosity. She strode to the bay window and looked out at the darkness. She even hated his name—Arjun! A sudden fear gripped her, a fear that her daughter might distance herself from her as the years grew by.

Though her eyelids were heavy with sleep, she stood by the window and wearily watched a nebulous dawn broaching the horizon. Her mind was restless. Finally, slowly beginning to feel dizzy, she walked up to her bedroom and curled in her bed. With the pillows hugged in her arms, Neema eventually got lost in the cradle of sleep.

She was there again in some unknown jungle. The tawny, flickering light of a distant lamppost winked laboriously under its terminal breath. She dragged him by the collar on the scarcely trod path, tied him to the trunk of a tree, and slumped herself on the demonic bunioned branches of an age-old banyan tree. The lone, sharp howl of a distant dog pierced through the eerie silence of the woods and echoed in the moist, chill wind.

She opened a liquor bottle, took a deep swig, and threw the remaining contents on his face. Somewhere, the owl hooted and the crickets hummed monotonously, ungracefully, provoking the cosmic sound of silence.

'You can never subjugate a woman, you fool,' she screamed out. 'Wake up to the fact that she is Shakthi.'

Chapter Sixteen

Neema woke up with a start. She could hear faint sounds from his room.

She sprang out of bed with a beating heart and tiptoed up the stairs. Strangely enough, the door was only half-closed. He was at his open cupboard, going through a file. She stood by the doorjamb and said point blank that she needed a divorce. He went about his work. There was nothing strange about his non-reaction.

'You heard me. Didn't you?' she asked pertinaciously.

He turned around and barked, 'What?'

'I said I need a divorce,' she spit back.

He got back to his work and rubbed the tip of his nose perfunctorily. 'Sorry. You have to discuss this with your mother,' he said nonchalantly.

'This is incredible! What has my mother got to do with this?' she exploded.

Her face reddened and she fumed with anger. She had the instinct to slap him with her bare hand or, still better, with the iron box that was on the iron board near his cupboard. But the consciousness that she was not as strong as him restrained her from advancing. She hung there, near the doorway. But he went about his task as if she were non-existent.

She went downstairs, shut the door of her room, and burst out sobbing.

Arjun took his mobile and whispered Neema's plight to Shravana with ecstasy.

'You did the right thing, buddy,' Shravana laughed aloud. 'You are a lawyer, so she expects you to file the divorce case. Never do that. You don't want the world to say that you have been unjust to your wife. Do you? She'll walk out shortly. Take my word for it. By the way, you are meeting me in the evening. Aren't you? I'll keep something ready for you.'

'You dirty idiot!' barked Arjun into the phone in a low, stifled tone, 'It was you who long back advised me to give her a baby so that the world doesn't think that I'm impotent, and now you are telling me not to file a divorce.'

'Aren't you held in high esteem by your black coat folks?' Shravana asked challengingly, 'Meet me in the evening!' He hung up the phone.

Within minutes, Neema heard the main door bang. She knew Arjun had left. She hurriedly got up and started to pack. She stuffed in some of Goldie's clothes, too, before she hurried to her college. She wanted to get out to someplace, at least for a couple of days, some beautiful, serene place, something of a hill station, neither very far nor very close to Bangalore. In the end, she chose Madikeri. She rushed home in the afternoon from her college and waited for Goldie's return from school.

As soon as Goldie arrived from school at half past three, Neema breathlessly announced that the two would be going off to Madikeri for a few days on a trip.

Goldie screamed with joy and ran up and down the stairs excitedly to pick up a story book or a dress that her mom might have forgotten to pack.

'How many days are we going to stay there?' she questioned eagerly with her cute, big grin.

'Maybe a week,' Neema replied in an unsure tone, locking the house in the twilight.

They hired a rickshaw to the busstand and boarded a private luxury bus. Goldie, who had a tiring day at school, sat by the window with a blanket drawn upand soon got lulled to sleep. Neema, sitting by herself in the AC coach, fell into a reflective mood while the bus switched off the lights and drove monotonously through the night streets of Bangalore.

#

Arjun met his friend Shravana late evening in his musty bachelor's apartment.

'So this is your surprise for me?' he punched Shravana's tummy sportively on seeing Priya and Tara already assembled there in their new outfits that the men had presented them with. Priya was clad in a transparent chiffon sari, exposing an anorexic body. Her highbrow and high cheek bones, a serpent-shaped orange tilak on her forehead, and long, coarse brown locks helped her showcase every inch of her vicious personality. Her gruff voice exposed much of her lewd behaviour. She threw her arms around Arjun's neck and hung there till he pressed his huge, slimy lips to hers. The four settled down with bottles of scotch and cigarettes to discuss the future.

When Arjun got up to leave, Shravana brought out a black rubber mask of a giant from his bag. 'This is the surprise!' he exclaimed with a big grin. Arjun took it and scrunched up his face, levering it against his eyes and examining it. 'What's this for?' he blinked, amused by the impish-looking face and the long, coarse-fibred black hair swept back from its forehead and hanging long and loose on either side of its terrifying face. It stared at Arjun heinously with its pair of bloodshot eyes grinning horrendously, showing its long, white teeth.

'Hoist this on a prop and keep it in the corner of the door in Goldie's room,' Shravana grinned in an ugly manner. 'If the girl is scared out of her wits and refuses to stay in the house, then your wife has to leave.'

They started to laugh and raised a champagne bottle.

'You have a Solomon's brain!' Arjun yelped in admiration and quaffed the contents of the bottle with overwhelming joy. He held the mask in an appreciative glance, studying it even more thoroughly, and pressed his eyes with his thumbs, seeking to squeeze out an overabundance of emotional happy tears. Finally, he coughed and hemmed to keep his overpowering jubilance under control. He took the mask and bid goodbye.

Priya joined him too. He dropped her at her working women's hostel—a hostel she had booked for herself to get away from her old professor husband whenever she wanted to have her own sweet time with Arjun. After dropping her off, he started his sixteen kilometre drive home through dark, narrow lanes in the night. He reflected on the things he would do after getting home. Goldie would be asleep. He would slipinto her room upstairs and prop up the mask in the corner between the wall and the door.

Gripped by a vague sense of happiness, he turned the key in the hole and got into the dark house noiselessly.

When he stepped into the vast dining hall, what presented itself to him was beyond his comprehension. He was flabbergasted to find Neema's room wide open. He quickly climbed up the stairs. Goldie's room, too, was wide open and empty, which suggested that they were gone. The instant thought that cropped up in his mind was *gone for good*, but the transitorysigh of relief wassoon ransacked by a rising suspicion that they couldn't have left forever. He slid open the doors of Goldie's cupboard. To his great disappointment, her schoolbooks and much of her belongings were there, intact. They would return, but tonight, on this decisive night, they were gone! He kicked the football at the door hysterically; it went rolling down the steps, lingered near the door of his own bedroom halfway down the stairs to the left, and then bounced down the steps and got caught between the legs of the dining table. The execution of his demonic plan had to be suspended.

He telephoned Shravana and raved madly with rage. 'Where the hell could they have gone?'

Disregarding Shravana's plea for patience, he banged his fist over the glass-topped corner table in his room and shattered it to pieces.

CHAPTER SEVENTEEN

After marriage, it was the first time Neema had ventured out on her own on an unknown journey. It was also the first time she had left without informing her husband. A feeling of anxiety clung to her nerves.

She closed her eyes to allay the growing disquietude, but thoughts of her agitated life occupied her mind. She turned her mind to Milan. Thoughts of him always brought a whiff of pleasure and a smile to her face. He loved her still. And she loved him too. *To be in his arms...* She opened her eyes and took in a deep breath. The AC was beginning to get too cold. She drew up the comforter and shifted her position. Through the tinted glass window, everything looked dark outside. She knew that the coach had left the city and was driving through the countryside with vast fields of crops on both sides of the road.

Goldie was in deep slumber; her head drooped towards the window. Neema held her daughter's head and tilted it towards her own shoulder with the unfathomable affection of a mother. She pulled the blanket up over Goldie's shoulders and tucked the edges of it safely at the back. She realised at that very moment that her intense longing to be with Milan had to be curbed. Seeking to find pleasure with him would only mean paying less attention to her daughter. She didnot want to do that. As such, Goldie was so alone. Without a sibling, without a loving grandma, without a caring dad, not even a loving aunt.

Neema leaned her head back and fell into contemplation. The train of her thoughts ran back to the alpha stage of her drab marital life.

Nervous and shy, on that nuptial night, she had meekly lain on the far end of the bed. Her left arm and leg pressed against the curtain of the window in that bourgeois house, which Arjun had rented in a locality she never knew about, somewhere far from the city centre.

A pale, hushed light of the quarter moon filtered through the curtain, making them dully visible to each other. He had lain with his arm over his eyes, but later in the quietdarkness, he had stretched out his hand and his fingers had slid over her upper arm.

'Try your best to act normal,' Shravana had advised him.

With the warm touch of Arjun's fingers, a wave of pleasant current had shot up her arm and quivered with happiness. He had raised himself on his elbows, breathing hard on her. She had coyly shifted her slender hip, happily and nervously and had moved closer to him, albeit feeling uncomfortable in her heavily brocaded wedding sari.

She remembered having snuggled close to him and put her arm around his neck. She had pulled herself up and kissed his brow, cheeks, and then all over his face and was holding her breath with rising passion when she had felt his warm hand on her navel, trying to pull out the tucked pleats of her sari. When he happened to press her breasts, she had gasped and choked and when his fingers stroked her loin, she had moaned with her eyes closed tight. He whispered something. She heard but had failed to comprehend.

He had repeated the words for a second time close to her ear rather annoyingly and she heard it: 'When did you have your periods?' he had said, a query that had suddenly made her sick, instantly draining out in its entirety the swelling passion that had set the clock of her body ticking unnaturally fast.

'A fortnight ago,' she heaved timidly.

'O, shit. I want no children yet.' He had plucked her hands off his body, rolled away from her, and had lain still with his arm on his brow. Shravana had taught him the game well.

Just when she was hankering for his warmth with swelling passion, these credulous, unwarranted words had blown it all like a bomb out of the blue. A dizziness of pain and insult—words that fell like a loop around her throat, throttling her. She had lain with shock and sadness, like a patient with dropping blood pressure in the dark.

The yearning, palpitating micro throbs in the million cells of her body had frozen within micro seconds like a zombie sent back to its crypt.

On other days for a few months, he lay a distance away from her with his arm crossed over his forehead, his eyes wide open, staring into nothingness in the dark that received a beggarly wash of the crescent moonlight through the curtained window, enough for her to realise that he was not asleep. Night after night, he seemed to be ruminating over something that she had no access to.

A year later on a cold December night, he had come home heavily drunk and grasped her wrist in the dark. 'Come closer,' he had whispered.

She had reluctantly outstretched her hand. His warm, thick index finger had glided down her cheek and then down her chest and had slid behind the neckline of her blouse. Neema had closed her eyes and had waited for his next move without responding as the pain of the nuptial night had clung to her like a leech. He was still a stranger to her.

With his warm, masculine touch, her heart had almost stopped its normal beating. His crisp full white sleeve had sent tremors up her loin. No sooner had he pressed his slimy lips to hers, he had hastily begun unbuttoning her blouse buttons and within seconds, he had pulled off his shirt, too. She had helped him a little in the stripping process though and had eventually felt him pushing into her. She lay under him and pretended to enjoy it, muffling the reviling sensation, feeling more pain than the enjoyment that she had so much looked forward to. Their first mating over, it had ended there. He had shifted to the other room, hardly bothering to give her an explanation in spite of her continuous questions and pleas.

Nine months later, she had given birth to Goldie and had revelled in the pleasure of her first born.

The bus suddenly halted for a loo break in front of a hotel that had bright lights and other tourist buses. It was quarter to four in the morning. It was still dark outside the periphery of the neon wash of street lights. Stars were still twinkling in the pre-dawn sky. She turned her head and looked at Goldie. She didnot want to wake up the child. She bent her head and gently kissed her girl on the brow with a contented smile, closed her eyes, leaned her head back on the head cushion of her seat, and waited for the bus to resume its journey.

CHAPTER EIGHTEEN

At half past five in the morning, they reached Madikeri.

The hill station was colder and damper than usual that July. Neema checked into a resort that had a row of independent cottages running down the hill, each neatly erected on square pieces of sod. In the front, a pea stone pathway snaked down the gradient grassy hill in a gentle curve and along it ran a flight of stairs with intermittent landings to pause and view the beauty of the surrounding landscape. A verdant lawn stretched far and wide and a short white compound wall in the distance demarcated the hotel property. Along the stretch running down the slope was a beautiful bed of a lively, coloured spray of flowers that presented a most scenic view which Neema and Goldie marvelled at, standing on one of the landings halfway down the steps.

A cheerful old gentleman, probably in his late sixties, greeted them heartily at the reception and said that he ran the business for the past few years after having retired from military service. He called an ayah to escort them to the plush cottage that was first in the row, promised to send them a complimentary kettle of Coorg coffee, and wished them good luck.

The wooden flooring, low ceiling, and the amazing view of the distant misty, serene hills and valleys from the window of Neema's cottage was breath-taking. This was the ultimate delight to Neema. Goldie peered out, awestruck, standing by her mama's side. With the satin curtain drawn to a side, they gazed out the tall, wide window and watched layers of undulating landscape, hazy and grey, shrouded by mist, basking in its tranquillity. Neema watched the obscure figures of a few women, their heads wrapped in colourful scarves, at work in the coffee plantation uphill, diagonally opposite her window.

They got breakfast served in their room and the two, mother and daughter, ate joyfully, watching a Hollywood movie on the television. Later, they played with pillows, danced and screamed and tickled each other, and finally crashed onto the thickest, softest mattress they had ever slept on.

Afternoon was spent walking through the coffee plantation and visiting a nearby temple and the rest of the day chatting with local people who pampered Goldie with peppy talk. Later that evening, they ate in their lovely resort restaurant that had an air of romance with dimly lit, beautiful little globes of bamboo chandeliers. They then strolled back to their cottage at nightfall.

When Neema woke up for a sip of water sometime around midnight, she stood by the tall window and watched the hushed silence outside. There were a multitude of stars shining in the dark, velvety sky. Yellow spots of twinkling lights could be seen on the rolling hills here and there that marked the tiny isolated cottages of the neighbourhood. Neema stood with the glass of water and pondered over the unique joys and pains that dwelt in the soul of each cottage out there. Myriad stories spawned and commissioned by the mysterious hand of the Divine above.

Morning greeted them with its enchanting beauty. A mild beam of sunshine kissed the lawn in its varied rainbow colours. The distant fog that hung on the valley was paradisiacal. A few men were already at work in the chill of the morn near her cottage, lifting barrels of sand and stone. A smile crawled on her mouth as she watched a few obdurate children playing marbles on the street. Suddenly, there were tears in her eyes. This was humanity struggling to realise unfulfilled desires, which could be even as small as eating chicken curry with rice and lentil cakes! She sighed deeply and settled on the couch with her morning cup of steaming hot coffee that had just arrived.

At noon, a cold gleam manifested through the grey, misty sky. She and Goldie were thrilled to wear their newly bought woollens. She showed her daughter rows of cardamom, nutmeg, orange and lemongrass crops and was glad that the trip also turned out to be an educational tour and noticed that Goldie was thoroughly enjoying it. They ate homemade chocolates and cookies and jackfruit chips sitting by a gushing mini waterfall that fell into a stream and meandered through a rocky hillock. They returned to their cottage and crashed for the day. Goldie was indeed so very happy!

When Goldie went to bed, Neema pulled out a covertly bought bottle of red wine from her handbag and stood by the window, looking out at the distant range of hills, silent and narcoleptic, charmingly visible under a bright gibbous moon. Sipping the wine leisurely, she watched the million glimmering lights of the valley below.

If only I had a mom to hug me and support me and understand me! She took a deep, long breath and gulped down the last dregs from the bottle. She stared at the darkness beyond the valley in the distance and wondered where her life was leading to without any friend or relative to empathise or sympathise with her.

The next morning, it had begun to drizzle. They were forced to stay indoors. They got food served in their room and in the dark noon sat by the glass window, watching the dreary day pass by, shrouded by mist. Thick, dark clouds raced beneath a light azure welkin. An effulgence of white clouds burst in the gloomy sky but receded with the same haste, playing hide and seek. Just as the day alternated with its gloom and gleam, Neema and her daughter played 'catch me if you can,' each taking the catcher's role in turn. They ordered for room service in the evening again, trolled all kinds of songs, danced and jumped and played word games until Goldie said she was sleepy. Neema, too, switched off the light and went to bed rather early, for it was a dark and chilly evening. She remembered Milan and longed to be in his arms until Hypnos lifted Neema in his affectionate arms.

Milan lay over her, kissing her cheeks and the nape of her neck. He made love to her gently in a cottage on the hills. She saw his beautiful, romantic, kind eyes looking down at her as she went down the hill and disappeared into the night. A steam engine chugged into a small, dark, queer-looking railway station in which she stood, holding on to her white wedding gown. Then there were other trains pulling into the station on other tracks. She hopped into one that had begun to chug. She was at its open door, holding onto its rail, speeding on an endless journey. The next moment, she was in her home standing naked in front of a mirror. Half-dressed urchins crowded around her, grabbing her hands and leading her away to the dark, wild chasm of some ancient cave.

She woke up with a vivid memory of her perplexing dream. Goldie had got up earlier than usual and was outside playing in the garden — on the carpet of tiny flowers of myriad hues. It was a bright and beautiful day, with cool breezy air. Gleaming droplets of water clung to the blades of the trembling grass and the dew-showered green shoots of the flowers quaked as Goldie skittered on the cool moist earth in her pink canvas shoes. Partially bloomed fleecy corollas of roses smiled under a blushing morning sky, iffy about its brightness for the day.

In the serene, lovely morning, Neema's thoughts wandered to Milan and the way he had made love to her in her dream.

While in the shower, Goldie called out and declared that she was missing her school and her friends. Neema considered it seriously with a little disappointment, as she didn't want to go home. It was but three days that they had ventured out on their own. A thought struck her to augment Goldie's curiosity. *Amere two and a half hour journey to Hassan by bus!* She was thankful for the idea that presented itself at the most appropriate situation. She announced their next picnic destination with much adulation, and Goldie was all curious again to visit her dad's birthplace.

CHAPTER NINETEEN

They started off the next morning, after breakfast. Her previous visit to Hassan had been with Arjun when they were newly married. She vaguely remembered the name of the street and could not recollect the exact location of the house, for there were other houses on the same street that had looked similar. She anticipated some difficulty in locating the house. When they alighted at Hassan's busstand, Neema's first reaction was one of confusion. She looked around and was dubious about her next course of action. She also wasn't sure of good hotels available in the town.

She knew the house would be under lock and key. Her parents-in-law were no more. They had died years ago. Father-in-law was the first after a gangrene operation and three years later, her mother-in-law had died of a heart attack in the arms of her faithful servant. And both times, Arjun was the only one who had made trips to Hassan.

While she hung around amid the numerous honking buses, hating to be exposed to the hot, muddy dust that rose from buses and rickshaws, one of the autos screeched in front of her and the young man in his khaki overcoat asked her if she needed a ride. She said Temple Street and got in with Goldie. He turned the throttle full and accelerated off, leaving behind the cluttered, hot, dusty busstand.

'Temple Street one or two?' he asked in a high pitch as they drove.

'Venkatswamy's house. Door number 33-D, if I'm right. Anyway that's the address. I think we have to look in both the streets,' she said hesitantly.

After a minute's thoughtful pause, the driver affirmed through the din of the motor, 'That's street number one. Nobody lives there, madam.'

'I know, but I want to see the house,' replied Neema unequivocally. She had promised Goldie that she would first show her the house.

He shrugged his shoulders callously and turned onto Temple Street One. Neema sat in consternation for a second. A frown gathered on her brow. How did he know that nobody lived in Venkatswamy's house?

Before she could ask him anything, she heard him speak again. 'Parents are no more, but Arjun sir visits occasionally. He is a lawyer. Practising in Bangalore.'

Neema grew alarmed. She took a long, deep, breath and found herself diffidently asking him in a tremulous voice, 'How do you know him? I mean, how do you know all this?'

'Ah-ha,' he guffawed and continued in a high pitch, 'that's a good question. I live on the same street. Know them inside out ever since I was six years old. He is married and lives luxuriously in the city, married to my mom's friend's daughter. We couldn't attend the wedding because it coincided with my father's annual death anniversary.' Neema was stupefied and the first thought that crossed her mind was *what if Arjun came to know of her visit to Hassan*. She was seized by a sudden sense of despondency, a surging flood of disillusionment and scepticism that almost seemed to block her thinking.

Her own bleak life was reflected to her in its metropolitan glory.

'This is Arjun's house,' the guy screamed in dissonance over the throttled engine.

'Papa's house! I want to go inside,' insisted Goldie, whose ears had propped up in curiosity. Neema was at a loss. She grappled with words and thoughts alike.

The young man watched her disgruntled composurein contemplation.—He turned around in a swivet and smiled at the girl. However, he was reluctant to accost a stranger.

Neema convinced Goldie that she would bring her there in the evening after lunch and rest.

'Any good hotels around?' she asked him, feebly traumatised by all that she had just heard from him. Thoughts assailed her in a way that exasperated her.

He asked hesitantly, half-turning around without meeting her eyes, 'Are you Venkatswamy's daughter-in-law, if I may ask so?' Neema was lost for an answer. He had just heard Goldie shriek, 'Papa's house,' which should have given him the cue. If she denied it point blank, it would, definitely, arouse his suspicions and to investigate the matter, he certainly would place a telephone call to Arjun.. On the other hand, if at all she acknowledged the truth, she might have to cover up a few facts tactfully. Even then, it would raise doubts as to the purpose of her visit and still the story might travel to Arjun's ears.

Forthwith, she decided to listen to her inner voice and said with sudden audacity, 'Yes, I'm Neema, Arjun's wife.'

He let go the throttle and clapped his hands, elated in his new discovery. 'You are Neema? I guessed so. You are not going to any hotel, sis. You are going to my house. Even your mom had stayed in my house for a night,' he said with a large grin.

'So, my mom, Kanthi, is your mom's friend?' she asked with a slight note of diffidence.

Though Neema was unsure about it, she didn't protest being taken to his house. Fate had thrown an opportunity her way to glean some information about her husband, which she had always wanted to know. An aleatory rendezvous that would give her an opportunity to learn things, which otherwise wouldn't come to light!

She flashed an unsure smile and Babu swirled his auto rickshaw around with genuine pleasure on his cute young face.

Jayamma was delighted to meet Neema and her daughter. She greeted them with utmost adoration and busied herself in preparing food. She asked Goldie what sweets she liked and what snacks she loved. She served them with servility and sat them on the newly bought cane chairs in the newly built annexe that made the antechamber, which they called the veranda. Jayamma's warmth and affection, the afternoon's cool breeze that wafted from the backyard orchard and the quietness of the place impressed Neema to an extent that she ventured to speak out, 'I didn't know my mom had a good friend like you here.'

'Actually, Neema, I was a cook . . .' Jayamma rambled the story of her yesteryears with Kanthi, of which Neema had not the faintest idea. Neema ogled and gobbled the story with utmost curiosity while Goldie played badminton with Babu in the front yard, crunching the brown dry leaves fallen everywhere from the various trees that grew there.

'So, tell me how's Arjun? It was I who proposed him to you. When your mom met him here, she was very much impressed by him,' Jayamma said in a somewhat victorious tone.

'So you were instrumental in finding me Arjun?' Neema asked, a little hurt, but she was discreet enough to cover it up with her cheerful tone.

'I bet he takes good care of you,' remarked Jayamma. 'Actually, he wasn't interested in marriage. I don't know how your mother turned him around. She is a wise woman, has always been.'

Neema faltered and said 'yes' faintly, with a quiet smile.

Babu came in pleased and exhausted and Goldie followed in, bouncing with merriment. Jayamma disappeared again, saying she would get them all some fresh coffee.

'Arjun sir has offered me a job in Bangalore,' Babu told Neema cheerfully without the faintest idea that she wouldnot know anything, while her heart sank in trepidation lest her visit to Hassan would be disclosed, now knowing that Arjun and Babu were in contact with each other.

'What job?' she managed to ask pleasantly.

'He says one of his friends needs an assistant. And he says I can share his friend's room that he has rented somewhere in Srinagar. But trust me; I'm going to come back to Hassan, because it's here where my heart is. I'm an entrepreneur here. I run my own auto rickshaw and I've my own house and my loving mother is comfortably settled here.'

In jest, he put his arms around the neck of his mother, who had come out with a tray of coffee. 'This boy is crazy about working in Bangalore for a while,' added Jayamma.

'I want to experience big city's life for a while,' adjoined Babu.

'Next year, he turns thirty-two and I want him to get married,' joked his mother. He gave out a big laugh. Neema spent the day chatting about a number of other things and decided to leave the next day.

Babu and Jayamma followed her to the gate at noon the next day, Babu wheeling her suitcase in one hand and holding Goldie's bag of fruits in the other. He had handpicked them all from his little orchard.

Neema got into the auto and just when he pulled the engine to life, she requested him to mute it for a minute in a dramatic gesture and beckoned Jayamma to come closer, as she had something to tell her. She said in an appealing tone, looking at both mother and son, 'Please don't tell Arjun or my mother about my visit here. My mother may hate me for not letting her know about my visit and Arjun, er, I haven't told him about my trip to Hassan because I was restless to show Goldie the place and Arjun has no time to accompany us.'

'I perfectly understand that,' Jayamma jibed and Babu nodded his head, conceding. He brought the engine to life again and lurched towards the busstand. He bought tickets for them, put them on the bus safely, and bid them goodbye.

When he came home that evening, he looked flushed and unusually fresh, in spite of a hectic day running the auto. He was humming a song after his food in the cool, moonlit front yard. When his mother came out for a breath of fresh air, he commented, 'That woman, Neema, looks no more than a college going girl. What do you say, Mom? She is very pretty and looks innocent. Like a flower in the garden,' he rambled.

His mother was flummoxed and understood the feelings that her son had succumbed to. 'Something wrong with you?' she questioned with a mixture of jest and sobriety and added as a cautious warning, 'She is Arjun's wife. Married with a teenaged daughter.'

'O, I know that, Mother. It's just that, er, ah! Just that . . . her dimple was cute. Cute and very attractive. She has a nice smile and . . .' He looked at his mother slyly and caught her gaze adjudicating him with an upturned corner of her mouth and narrowed eyes. He eyed her contemplatively and said, throwing up his arms, 'She is my sister, okay?' Jayamma smiled to herself and went in with a nod of her head.

Neema returned to her house with a peculiar hollowness in her bosom, feeling empty within, and turned the key of her empty house just when the cool air of a dying afternoon was reflectingthe already subdued sun. Twilight had taken the reins of the day.

She propped up her legs and sat upstairs on the cool windowsill in Goldie's room with a cup of steaming coffee that warmed her palms more than her insides. She sat with a pale countenance, looking out the window at the silent, empty field in the distance against the twilight horizon while Goldie went to sleep. Her moods changed like the little rippling waves of the stream, alternating between happiness and sadness, sending ripples of an unexplainable vacant and hollow feeling.

So Arjun had not been interested in marriage, but her mother had been able to turn him around?

But why had she gone to the extent of taking that trouble? Why had she influenced him to get married?If only Dad had known about all this!

A vague feeling of being cheated haunted Neema like a choking clasp around her throat. She bent her head over her locked palms, which rested on her folded knees and tried to stifle a gushing sob.

It had been a trip that had brought her a sense of freedom and joy; the hospitality of Jayamma and that of her son's was something she couldn't forget. It was also a trip that had thrown light on a few things she didn't know about.

She rose and climbed down the stairs dully. An aphonic weariness clung, leech-like, lending its unbearable agony in which her once-effusing spirit now seemed to have drained out in its entirety. A passive, unfathomable emptiness seized her: spasmodic pain in her loin, gagged breaths, implacable depression. If anything, her hope for a better tomorrow zeroed to a naught.

She climbed up again, watched Goldie smile in her sleep, and perched herself on the windowsill again. The sole option of having to return to the same large, cold, empty house brought gushing tears that rolled and dropped to her lap from her beautiful, pallid eyes.

Her mother's disappearance that cold morning without letting even Dad know about her trip also made sense now. It became certain to Neema now that her mother had rushed to Hassan, and that the discussion with Arjun had been kept a secret.

As she sat there, her mind drifted to memories of herclose college friends and the last time they had all gotten together at Lily's house. The bitter truth of Lily's solitariness and her angst in a huge mansion without anybody of her own took on a new meaning now.

Chapter Twenty

That morning, when Kanthi had gone off to Hassan, Neema had woken up to the appetizing aroma of rasam that was wafting from the kitchen. There was a peculiar silence in the house. The sun was already bold and bright outside. But there was no sound of her mother's nagging. Mom wouldn't have let her sleep that long. Even during periods when passion rode high on her nerves and lethargy brooded on her bones, Neema was made to get up early.

But that day, the clock had struck eight, yet the house was so quiet!She got up apprehensively and walked into the hall timidly. There was no one there. While trying to tiptoe to the bathroom, she caught sight of her dad in the kitchen. That was amazing! She stood at the doorway with a surprised smile. There couldn't have been anything more surprising than that! It was an eventful day for her.

Her dad turned his head around and spoke with a big smile 'Got up, honey?Go and wash yourself. I'll give you a fresh cup of coffee.'

'Mom is not at home, Dad?' she asked gently.

'God knows where she went; she didn't inform me, though. Mili should know.' He was speaking with his back turned. He didn't sound upset. Neema had no further questions. She was just elated that her star had changed its spot in the morose dark cloud.

She heard Dad calling out Mili's name. 'A nice, hot cup of coffee! Come quick and get it. It's getting late for me.'

'Where did your mom go?' he finally asked the reticent girl dispassionately while tying his shoes.

'What do I know?' she said irately. 'She only told me that she would be back soon.'

He stood up, put on his belt, and left. Neema disappeared into her room to enjoy her day reading a romantic novel.

Lying cosily in bed, she dreamt of a Romeo with whom she would spend her entire life in a neat, tidy little cottage in the woods. He would come home and hold her little waist and she would give in to his passionate kisses. She would clean and keep up his house, cook tasty dishes for him, wash his tired feet, and would never be afraid of darkness or loneliness with a loving Romeo in her life. She dreamt of sex and romance and the gifts they would exchange, and she rolled in her bed, squeezing pillows around her.

A slanting sheet of rain had started to beat mercilessly against the pane. Neema picked up her favourite, *Jane Eyre*, rolled into her bed again, and listened joyfully to the drone of the lashing rain. She loved it. The elated feeling of being so free and liberated, at last, for once in her life had overcome her in its ecstasy. She mixed herself a steaming cup of coffee with lots of creamy milk as evening drew on and began to read the latter part of *Jane Eyre* in her bed, where Rochester gets passionate with Jane.

Her mother having gone had given her all respite and liberty, which she had always looked forward to so much.

Later in the evening, she made hasty calls to her dearest friends and with squeaks and giggles suggested that they all meet the next morning at Lily's place. Her suggestion had been too thrilling for any of them to reject, and they all acquiesced with happy screams and laughter and the four girls had been restless all night for the new dawn to broach. Her rendezvous with Lily and the rest of her friends for the last time had been then, a month before her marriage

Lily's huge, beautiful house, the little flowery garden in the front yard with a gazebo, and the balcony with the cushioned iron swing with awning—everything had been a source of mild jealousy mixed with pleasure that Neema silently hid. But all the same, she loved Lily. Not just Lily. The others too! A strong, unremitting bond had been established among the four girls. They all gathered promptly at Lily's house for breakfast the next morning. Their strong, committed friendship had not at any time given any room for any kind of vitriolic thoughts or feelings. Lily was in a peculiarly high spirit that day and the rest, exuberant, were in tandem with her.

Sitting in the breezy gazebo, the four girls discussed their future and disclosed their thoughts. Aparna announced that she had decided to elope with Aziz. Parentless since the age of fifteen, her elder brother and sister-in-law had been her guardians and they disapproved of her boyfriend who was a Muslim. Moreover, he was a native of Orissa, making it all the more difficult for either of their families to accept each other.

Neema was staring into the air between the shoulders of Sneha and Aparna, mutely reflecting over the gap that had been created between her and her mother. She quietly announced that she had finally resolved to get married and that she would raise no protests to her parents' choice.

'Don't make resolutions like that,' Sneha warned. 'Marrying a stranger and making a hasty decision can mean jumping from the frying pan into the fire.'

'Marriage is a gamble. Whether your decision is hasty or prolonged, what has to happen will happen,' Neema argued.

'No!' Aparna said resolutely. 'I feel we can shape up our destinies. Now you see, I love this guy, Aziz. To abandon him now just to please my brother and then getting married to someone, I wouldn't like, will be a lifelong regret. I love Aziz and I'm going to get married to him. That's it.'

Sneha burst the big, pink bubble of her chewing gum, as she listened to them intently and, without looking particularly at any one of them, avouched, 'I don't agree with either of you. When it comes to marriage, of course, love is important, that being the first point. But before one plunges into anything, careful thought must be given to the choice one makes, so that you take responsibility for whatever happens to you in the future and don't blame others for what happens to you.'

Lily, who had been a listener, broke her silence, 'Whatever,' she said. 'Fate, destiny, luck, gamble, blah, blah ... Life is all just about being happy. If you are not happy, you are doomed. You won't even have the strength to shape up your destiny. I don't believe in fate, either. It's just that, whether you have the strength to live your life the way it is. Survival of the fittest and ...'

'Uuuuuu ...' the girls clapped their hands and hooted in approbation like they always did whenever Lily said anything. But she always took it cheerfully for she knew their angelic hearts and thoughts that they carried with them. She was a year younger and was treated like the baby of their group.

'Let's not waste time anymore.' Sneha jumped up zippily, looked at Lily, and said, 'Show us your new dresses, darling.' Lily, excitedly, led them in, into her room and pulled out all of her stylish dresses from her cupboard. 'Here starts our fashion show!' she declared and started stripping. 'C'mon and grab whatever you want,' she insisted and set up the cassettes that played Western hip hop. There were dresses which she hadn't even tried. There was screeching, dancing, and stripping with peals of laughter, mimes, and mimicries, and the girls began their unique fashion show.

For the first time, Neema realised that, undoubtedly, she looked stunningly pretty in those fashionable dresses with her soft curls let loose. Halter-neck frocks, silk party gowns, bottle tops, velvet outfits and oh! She was thrilled to the highest degree—all bought from Singapore, Hong Kong, or Taiwan.

'Girl, you look pretty. Really pretty,' Lily had cried and burst out laughing upon seeing Neema struggling with a black stretch top, frantically searching for its sleeves while standing in her bra and panty. 'What kind of dress is this?' Neema had screamed out, exasperated, and the rest were in splits, unable to even breathe, rolling on the bed holding their tummies. Finally, Neema too had thrown herself on the bed, choking with rib-aching laughter.

'I give up,' she had declared, rubbing her nose with her handkerchief. 'That dress of yours is stupid. The head portion looks like knickers; the sleeves look like panties. Well, I don't even know how to get into it.' She changed into her own salwar kameez and said, 'That piece is really funky. It looks like a baby's nappy. Oh God, which is the neck and where are the sleeves?' And again, they were all choking with laughter.

Sneha and Aparna had resumed their exit and entry from the adjacent little room on stilettos and goggles in different styles, as if they were walking down the ramp in a fashion show, and there was so much of fun and laughter for them all to remember for a lifetime. The girls were blinded with tears until the cheerful maid announced that snacks and tea were waiting for them.

Honey cake, fruit cake, French fries, crackers, samosas, cutlets, and tea were all served in the most expensive china cups and trays, which the girls were fascinated with. Neema dreamt of owning them one day.

Later, when they all sat on the balcony, Neema threw up her hands for attention and sang Rudyard Kipling's poetry lines with her own adaptation, 'Ah, Hindus are Hindus and Muslims are Muslims and never the twain shall meet, Till Earth and Sky stand presently at God's great Judgement Seat.'

Aparna was quick to banter, 'But there is neither Hindu nor Muslim religion, Border, nor Breed, nor Birth, when two lovers stand united, tho' they come from the ends of the earth!'

Neema began to laugh so hard that her tea got into her windpipe and the rest were all shaking with laughter again till tea was spilling onto the floor.

 In the evening, rocking themselves on the swing in the cool balcony, they watched with ennui as the red orb in the beautiful orange horizon quickly sank somewhere behind the sheath of sky, bidding adieu, its day over.

Lily suddenly declared with a sudden change of her mood that life had no charm for her. The girls were utterly shocked. Their gaze had suddenly turned to Lily.

Despondency sat on her countenance as if it had come to stay there. Suddenly disassociated from her surroundings, Lily was looking blankly at the horizon. Neema shook her to her present self, threw her arms around her neck, and begged her to cheer up. 'We are always with you. Your life is not as bad as mine!'

But Lily had protested. 'No, Neema. Right from my school days, I've been alone,' she said gloomily. 'You know that my mom died of cancer when I was eight and my dad is always travelling. None of my relatives drop by or have ever bothered about me. They think material riches is everything and they are jealous. My maid is a darling, of course. But I've none to call my own. I've always been so alone. And you are getting married shortly. I'm gonna miss you. Sneha is going away too to Delhi to do some business, and Aparna running away with Aziz.' She threw her glance with a sigh at Aparna, who threw her arms around her and said, 'I'm always here for you, darling Lily.'

'I've never had anyone to comfort me in my life,' Lily continued. 'That boyfriend I quit with last year was a great flirt. No, no, Neema. There is no love on this earth like we dream of,' she had said dejectedly, turning to Neema.

Sneha and Aparna chided her for speaking rubbish and Neema consoled her, saying, 'I'm always here for you. I bet you will get married to the best guy. We are here, your friends! We are all going to be present for your wedding.'

Her marriage had never taken place. Tears welled in Neema's eyes now. Still sitting on the windowsill in Goldie's room, enveloped in midnight darkness, Neema felt bitter and bereaved for having travelled down this memory lane.

Lily never turned up for Neema's marriage, which took place the following month. Neither did Aparna nor Sneha. It was assumed that Aparna had eloped as she had said, and nothing was known about Sneha. Their telephones were unreachable.

And when Neema telephoned Lily's home, it was the maid who broke the bad tidings through uncontrollable sobs that Lily had consumed some poison and had been found dead in her bed just the previous evening. However, she said that the girl had left a beautiful framed picture of Mother Mary and Jesus for Neema as her wedding gift.

Neema deeply missed them all, especially Lily, cognizant of the fact that she would never see her again. She couldn't brush away memories of Lily. She softly climbed down the stairs, curled up in her own bed, and quickly succumbed to the mighty Hypnos. A strange dream rolled out.

Neema was pregnant and was with her friend, Lily. They met at the soulless, empty crossroads lit brightly by a single tall lamppost at the town centre in the dead of night. Standing about fifty metres apart, they stared into each other's faces, pale smiles lighting up their eyes, both thinking of spotting a maternity hospital somewhere in the vicinity. Suddenly, as if they had unanimously hit upon a hospital, they nodded to each other and started walking down, abreast, through a forlorn, muddy road, with their shadows trailing behind them in the dim whiteness of a distant moon. They turned at a corner into a wide, dark, silent road and walked on the sand in their bare feet in loose, full-sleeved white gowns till they came upon an enclosure, vast and barren, its compound walls stark white in the stygian darkness. Two modest-looking buildings, also stark white, stood isolated and desolate a hundred metres away in the dim light of the distant stars, their hushed facades facing each other, each of them with a flight of three broad steps with little white sidewalls. All windows and doors were sealed, with no sign of life, whatsoever. The girls leaned against the short compound wall and took in the dark vastness of the hushed, lonely atrium when all of a sudden two short, old, haggard nurses emerged from the dark void and stood in the centre of the paddock in their immaculate white uniforms. Their wrinkled eyes fixed on the girls. And in a flash, Neema was there, inside the atrium, between them, transformed to a child holding their hands. The three stood staring at Lily, while she hung there, outside the wall, watching them turn around and disappear into the night. She bid farewell to her friend, Neema, before she vanished.

Chapter Twenty-One

Months tumbled and years heaved by and chucked out the daily trammels of Neema's lonely life until one fine day, she felt sick and feverish.

Whether she divorced Arjun legally or not didn't matter much. *A divorce would facilitate another marriage, but I'm not in love with any man,* she told herself.

Nor did Arjun raise the divorce topic. Kanthi and Shravana had advised him not to. 'What if she comes to me for her share of property?' Kanthi had fumed and Shravana had diligently questioned him, 'What if she stands by Goldie, who is a major now, and fights legally for the huge, ancestral property of which you are the king now?'

Arjun, on his part, kept promising Priya that he would marry her soon. 'You have a husband too,' he told her. 'Wouldn't it be better to have our spouses uprooted once and for all from the face of the earth?' He would make her smile with the idea and press her to his bosom.

Neema no longer had the inclination to go to a workplace that lacked elements of warmth or affection, appreciation or encouragement, friendliness or oneness. Neither was there a challenging and professional atmosphere. Those aspects remained a far cry in a setup where people simply slogged with long faces for monetary benefit. She preferred to stay in the confines of her silent house rather than confront a friendless, harsh world.

Swaddled in a blanket of disinterestedness, she chose to retreat into her own private world. She felt secure indoors with the lingering consciousness that she had to survive, no matter what, for her daughter's sake, who otherwise would become an orphan.

Wrapped in a shawl and with coffee in her hand, she watched the world go by with a scowl, through the big, tinted glass of the living room window. Swathed in an implacable ennui, she stood behind the glass, blank and lost, with a lump of sadness occluding her throat. She did not want to shed tears anymore. She would rather let the hollow sensation of depression fester within rather than vent it out to no use. That was her upturned harsh resolution.

Popping analgesics to allay her pathological aches became more frequent. She would turn around from the window and meet the cool emptiness of the living room with a wicked smile. Except for the cream sofa set on her side, a few inches away from the window, and the television set at the far end, perched on a hexagonal wooden stool under the elliptic flooring of the upper hall, the vast living room otherwise looked ghostly barren.

At times, she climbed the chill, white marble stairs absent-mindedly and stood with her hands on the arced iron railing of the upper hall that overhung the living room down below. She would then enter Goldie's room to gaze for a while through the window at the distant field.

Possessed by Oizys, with her head drooping, she would dawdle, at times, to the kitchen, rabidly hungry even before a shower, and tarry near the gas stove. Her mind far removed from the immediacy, she would reach mechanically for the glass jug of the coffee maker, pour the decoction into a china cup that was exclusively hers, mix sugar and milk, and hobble to the living room, sometimes with a tray of dry cookies or cold rice and yoghurt with some pickle.

Sometimes, when she continued to idle away on the couch, a subtle, ironical smile would catch the corner of her little mouth as the bitter irony of her marriage would come flooding into her mind. With involuntarily distended nostrils, she breathed deep and long and saw it all, her wasted life, livid in agony, while a hint of a frown would stealthily rise on her brow as she stared into nothingness.

Neema's beautiful, dull eyes which seemed to be shelved into little weeping islands hardly batted, s she slouched and stared dumbly at the muted channels, dully surfing again and again in a benumbed hope of running into something interesting. Yet again, she would lapse unknowingly into a chimerical world, watching events that she had confronted in the journey of her life while she fought to keep at bay the swelling tide of the strong ocean of tears that leapt in her throat, in the melange of feelings and thoughts that she was drowning in.

She picked up the remote one afternoon while the midden lay rotting on the kitchen counter, pressed the auto search button, and settled down with her food. Funny, abrupt sounds popped and died in mono and di syllables as she surfed. They scurried successively with bright flashes of colour. Surfing again and again from channel one, monotonously and disinterestedly gripped by sadness, she chanced upon something that suddenly caught her attention.

It was one of those Bollywood movies. But the scene was a special one, something that suited her mood. The hero and the heroine, Bobby Deol and Amisha Patel, were engrossed in their own micro-cosmic world of love and heartfelt repentance for their past mistakes. Neema was transfixed with an emotion, not one of negative bitter feelings for the lack of that kind of heartfelt love in her own life or jealousy, but paradoxically, it was one that negated the absinthial feelings she was so wound up with. Pulling up her legs, she sat in a more comfortable position. Sitting cross-legged on the wide couch, she watched the scene with such absorbing intensity that she began to feel composed and peaceful, as if it had salved her conscience. A flicker of smile swam in her tired eyes. At last, she moved her hand and scratched her sallow cheek and tucked her dishevelled hair behind her ears. She peered at the name of the movie that flashed on the top left corner of the screen. It read *Humraaz*.

Such caring, intense, and intriguing love! She would give anything for it. She took a deep breath and watched the whole movie for the first time in many years until twilight hijacked daylight.

The film over, she got up in a lighter mood, stretched herself, and went to the kitchen. She cleaned up the countertop and almost back to her normal self, filled her tray with buttered toast and a pot of coffee, and climbed up the stairs. She stood on the balcony and enjoyed her snack for the first time after many days and watched, with pleasure, children playing on the street even after nightfall. The beautiful night sky was not black at all. It looked lit from within. She couldn't say whether it was the light of the hidden moon or reflection of the city lights. She didn't give a damn. The sky was just so calm and cool with a wash of pale white light, sprinkled with minute, twinkling stars. She turned her gaze from the lovely sky to the scooty peps that came down the street. Goldie had not yet arrived. She was nineteen and a college girl. She finally sat in the rattan chair under the darkening sky and conjured Bobby Deol. The sentimental songs of the movie kept repeating in her brain.

When Goldie returned, she hugged and kissed her and promised to prepare her favourite dishes for her next day's dinner, and the girl promised that she would be home earlier the next day.

Sitting in the twilight breeze in her cushioned rattan chair almost became a routine for Neema. She sat in tranquility and hummed the plaintive lines of 'Humraaz.' She wondered where Milan was, but she knew nothing of him. She clung to her imagination that had begun to weave romantic dreams. She would run into Bobby's arms in her visual fantasies. The movie had helped her spring back to her former self again with grit and passion and she was, for good or bad, twirling in the whirl of love and fantasia to which she had surrendered.

She went back to work. It was more than a fortnight since she had been on hiatus.

Waiting for her classes to get over was something she looked forward to eagerly. She wanted to watch all of Bobby Deol's movies. It seemed to her like he had the power to fortify her sinking spirit.

Ah! To have a husband like that! She would heave a pathetic sigh. She needed no better nepenthe than the phantasmal world she resorted to. She sat in her bed and delved into the feelings that were gripping her. Was she in love with this actor, Bobby? But Milan was there who had expressed his love for her, and she had rejected him. Reflecting over it, she felt safe in her phantasmal world. She rented all of Bobby Deol's movies and watched them with zest. She was at liberty to retreat into her own shell of gratifying passion. She had discovered a tranquilising world, narcotic and analgesic.

She took her diary and wrote:

> *O, man!*
>
> *I love the sound of your laughter,*
>
> *Your gait, your voice and YOU, of course!*
>
> *I see you in my dreams,*
>
> *And those dreams are solely mine.*
>
> *Nobody shall invade them, snatch them, or stride on'em.*

Is reality better than dreams?

No, not for me of course!

I love the dreams I dream on breezy, sunny afternoons

Sitting on my windowsill, looking at the distant fields,

Sometimes on my swing on cool, dark evenings

Watching the racing clouds of a stormy night.

My silent dreams can hurt no one

Nor will it ever tread on another's heart

Only to stand up and curse me in agony.

Oh, Bobby! Who else can understand

the degree of your vengeance and wrath,

But for me, when your virtuous love has failed.

She was more cheerful than ever before. Coming home was not drudgery anymore. She wept and watched his movies repeatedly. Who else, but Bobby? Only he would understand the hatred she bore for her husband! She basked in her thoughts and greeted the mornings with little smiles.

CHAPTER TWENTY-TWO

On a Sunday morning, when Arjun was lying naked with Priya and Shravana in the peak of sexual pleasure, he received Neema's message on his mobile that said she was leaving immediately to Rajajinagar, since her mother had been admitted to the hospital. By the time Neema arrived in the hospital, Kanthi had been transferred to the ICU. Neema was permitted to only peep through the glass.

Mili, who was already there, told her, 'Yesterday evening, we went to visit Mom and stayed overnight. This morning, she slipped and fell in the bathroom and became unconscious. My husband and I have brought her to the hospital here. We will be glad if you could stay here till we are back, as my husband and I need to go home for a while.'

Neema readily agreed and stood outside the closed glass door and sighed tearfully. *Poor Mom!* Her thoughts went numb with pity and sadness. Her mom was paralysed in her limbs. As Mili and her husband left, she sat on a soft-cushioned chair outside in the immaculately clean corridor of the private hospital and got lost in deep grief.

The fact that Kanthi could never make the picture-perfect mother of her school moral science book, which Neema had all along yearned for, brought back to her mind the day when Kanthi had grabbed her by the hair early one morning, while Neema, who had her monthly menses, was wrapped up in a mounting sexual urge and was soaking the warmth of its feeling in a half-awake state and had been unable to wake up promptly to the sharp ringing of the alarm. Such emotional urges usually gripped her when she had her periods and the lady psychologist doctor had explained to her that it was a natural phenomenon among adolescents.

Minutes ticked by in her reverie. Sometime in the afternoon, she spotted Arjun entering the corridor. He threw a glance at Neema and walked towards the ICU. Kanthi spotted her son-in-law peering through the glass door.

Mili joined them a few minutes later and hovered near the door of the ICU. Standing behind her brother-in-law, she looked at her mother in silent pity. Mili did not make any attempt to talk to Neema, nor did the latter, who had confronted all the bitter experiences of her life single-handedly.

The doctor said that it would take months before Kanthi would be able to move. However, he said that he couldn't make definite promises. Neema overheard Mili telling Arjun that she had arranged for a full-time nurse to be with her mom. Satisfied with what she had heard, she left silently. A wave of aloneness had gripped her unaccountably. She suddenly had the urge to be with her sweet, little, innocent daughter.

#

Babu had taken up his new assistant job with Shravana a few months ago and had come to stay in Bangalore. He hadn't married yet, as he hadn't found a suitable partner. Tired of running an auto rickshaw in a small town, he had finally decided to try his luck in a bigger city in a bigger venture, and he had set his heart on opening a restaurant in Bangalore. With the burgeoning population of Bangalore, he had started to dream of big money.

He longed to visit Neema, but abstained from taking such a bold step. Arjun had never invited him home. The fact that he had met her could not be revealed to Arjun. However, a week after his arrival, he had telephoned her with elated pleasure and informed her that he had arrived in Bangalore and that he was staying with Shravana, her husband's best friend.

As the weeks rolled on, Babu realised that his boss stayed in the apartment only during weekends and occasionally for a day or two during the week.

Babu was introduced to Tara and Priya as office secretaries and Arjun teased his ladylove, in front of Babu, of being a wealthy, spoilt girl, and as being the only daughter of a rich land owner in Madikeri. Babu took upon himself the pleasure of cooking for all of them during the weekends. The fact that he was provided with accommodation in a big, expensive city like Bangalore became a valid reason for Babu to get himself engaged in such a service, a service which he genuinely enjoyed, besides being Shravana's office assistant.

A few weeks later, surprisingly Arjun did not show up on a particular Saturday when Babu had sought permission from Shravana to cook a lavish dinner, as it was Priya's birthday. Shravana was equally surprised, but when he made calls to Arjun, they weren't answered. Nor could they reach Priya.

They didn't hear from him for the entire week. But on Friday evening, the thought weighing on Babu heavily, he attempted to ask Shravana, while serving him his favourite food, if he had heard anything from Arjun.

Shravana didn't answer immediately. Clad in a sleeveless white banian and checkered lungi, which he had gathered between his knees, he kept eating and relishing his food, watching the television.

Arjun had not informed him about his whereabouts for the first time. He guessed that Arjun might be travelling with Priya. But where the hell they had gone had not come to his understanding. He was indeed angry with Arjun.

'Arjun sir has not turned up for so many days. The other day, he only told us that he was visiting Kanthi Aunty since she had a fall,' Babu said.

'What about it?' Shravana said grimly at length while Babu, regretting having been too nosy, pretended not to have heard. He loitered in the kitchen for a few extra minutes, noisily fidgeting about with the tongs, for he believed that it was not his business to delve into his bosses' personal lives.

When he came out, Shravana said, 'That ragged head is just fine. And I'm sure, if something had happened to Kanthi, he surely would have telephoned and informed us.' After a while, he said, 'Why don't you telephone and find out?'

'Yeah, but you sure, you know nothing, sir?' Babu asked with a smile and cleaned up the table on which the boss had eaten.

'You do one thing,' Shravana said. 'Telephone him and tell him that I'm continuously complaining about his absence and that I'm extremely upset.'

Babu gleefully carried out the errand. The next noon, he did as he was instructed. Arjun readily agreed to come in the evening and the bachelor's room turned once again into a sneaky place of laughter, plots, liquor, and cigar smoke.

However, Arjun was discreet enough not to disclose his visit to Madikeri. After Dasappa's brother's poisoned death, Shravana had warned him against visiting Madikeri at least for another few years.

Nevertheless, during this secret visit, Dasappa had unofficially declared Arjun as his son-in-law and as the future heir to all his property in the presence of a group of friends. It was Priya's birthday and she was delighted to be exchanging engagement rings with Arjun over a fabulous feast that her father had organised.

They even visited Hassan before they returned to Bangalore the night before Babu made the telephone call.

When they all gathered in the dingy room, Shravana looked at his friend, Arjun with suspicious eyes and noticed the new diamond ring on his finger, but checked himself against probing because Arjun had preferred not to open up.

Babu, as usual, confined himself to the kitchen, preparing a huge dinner with pleasure for all of them. When he came out of the kitchen to place the dishes and water, what he saw appalled him. He had least expected such a behaviour from Arjun sir, for whom he had the utmost reverence and admiration.

Priya had climbed onto Arjun's lap with her arms around his neck, and their lips were locked, her boobs pressed to his chest. Arjun, heavily drunk, had become unmindful of the presence of Babu.

Babu was knocked out of his wits. He looked at them, aghast, and disappeared into the kitchen in dismay. His heart began to pound. Something was not right. He had presumed Arjun, whom his mother had proposed for Neema, was a clean and respectable person. Back in Hassan, people thought that he was a good husband and a virtuous man.

All that Babu had come to know during his stay there was that the girls were officially appointed secretaries and joined the men for a drag and a little alcohol now and then to kick off their office blues, as was the customary habit of modern folks in big cities.

But that August evening, the truth stared Babu in the eyes. The reason for Arjun not accompanying his wife and child to Hassan dawned on Babu now. He now understood why even after so many years of marriage, Arjun had never brought his wife or child to Hassan but instead spawned stories that Neema was busy with the child and her college. It was over four months now that he had come to stay with Shravana, yet he hadn't been exposed to the truth. He felt ashamed for having been so foolish. He didn't know a thing about it till then— about Arjun's nasty life! It became pretty much clear to him now why he was sent off to films and ashram lectures now and then, especially on weekends!

He had been given to understand that Priya was the daughter of one Mr Dasappa, the richest landlord of Madikeri. Priya was spoilt, as Arjun had put it. Leaning against the counter in the small kitchen, he was suddenly overwrought with a number of worrying thoughts as he thought of Neema.

Arjun sir could have put her off. Shamelessly, he had given into the bimbo's passion! Was it possible that he was attracted to her money? Was it Priya's mistake in successfully ensnaring Arjun, or was it the latter's mistake in getting foolishly ensnared by a worthless character? What kind of life could Neema be leading? The innocent girl who he was extremely fond of! How could Arjun do this to her? Did she know about this? Was she shedding tears helplessly, or had given up on this? How could he cheat Neema, who was so pretty, young, and charming?

The longing to hold Neema in his arms swept Babu off his feet for a brief while, but he was quick to come back to his senses. A number of questions and thoughts assailed him as he lay that night in the dark. He was deeply perturbed by what he had seen. A sudden fatigue and anxiety weighed heavily upon him. He couldn't sleep, though. While Shravana snored heavily on his cot, Babu rolled, sleepless, with his eyes open, thinking about Neema's plight.

He recalled her ignorance about her mother's visit to Hassan.

Would Kanthi aunty know about Arjun's behaviour? Was Kanthi aunty regretting her visit to Hassan to make such a man her son-in-law? Could that be the reason for not having revealed to Neema of her visit to Hassan? Was she sick now because of the pain she was suffering? Was she regretting that she had got her daughter married to such a person?

Babu got up and noiselessly went out to have a drag. He sat on the steps in the cool night breeze with a million dusty stars twinkling above helping him to formulate a course of action he earnestly wanted to embark on: to save Neema from getting cheated further. His only goal was to help Neema get back her husband and get back all the happiness she had lost. He went in, noiselessly picked up Shravana's small telephone diary that was on the writing table, and riffled through the pages for Priya's number. Not able to find it on any page, he put the diary back in its place and went to sleep.

In the morning, he wasted no time in conveying to his boss about his decision to return to Hassan. He said that he had received a phone call from his mother saying that she was ill and hence it had become necessary for him to get back immediately. But when he read in the paper that a strike had been called by bus employees, he was forced to postpone his going by a day.

He got up early the next morning, prepared the day's meal for Shravana, typed out the few official documents that were kept on the table, packed himself some food, and left.

Chapter Twenty-Three

At a time when Neema didn't want anybody to disturb her tranquillity and peace, she was dismayed that there was someone at the door that Sunday afternoon when she was watching another of Bobby's movies.

A frown stood on her brow. *Who had dared to intrude at such an odd time of the day when many other housewives would actually be enjoying a siesta?* The few knocks on the door were followed by a firm ding dong of the bell. Arranging her dishevelled hair and salwar kameez quickly and wearing a smile to look modestly happy, she strode to the door with concealed annoyance and opened it to find a beautiful, fashionable woman about her own age, grinning at her, clad in a pair of blue jeans, a short purple top, and an unruly bunch of hair clipped high up, with beautiful curls swinging on either side of her thin, pretty face. She gazed at Neema from above her pink sunglasses with a naughty smile.

Neema's austere look, however, did not deter this young woman from speaking in the same old intimate manner the girls had adopted as established friends years ago on the campus.

'Hi, baby, you don't seem to recognise me,' she said softly and cheerfully, clutching at her zippy-looking shoulder bag with her slim, beautiful fingers that flaunted designer nails.

'Don't tell me that I have changed a lot!' she snickered on seeing Neema's confused half smile, 'What's my rebellious girl doing?'

The catch was in the long-forgotten appendage this young woman employed in her prying question. Years ago, while on the university campus, Neema remembered that she had been labelled as a 'rebellious girl'. With twinkle in her eyes, Neema stared at the woman with her mouth agape. The hint of recognition that alighted on Neema's face prompted the woman to throw her arms around Neema's neck. 'I'm Sneha. You rebellious girl!' she screamed out jubilantly.

Neema's senses shifted from aloofness to one of intimacy. She let out a cry of joy and threw her arms around her friend's neck. Interlocked jubilantly on the threshold for over a minute, they wiped their tears before Neema ushered her in with exuberant joy, her annoyance having evaporated in the air. Sneha flung her sassy handbag on the centre table and crashed onto the couch. 'Made a two-hour drive, baby, to see you,' she said boisterously and twittered endlessly, narrating her how she had unknowingly befriended a lecturer who worked in the same college in which Neema worked and how in the course of their conversation, she had stumbled upon Neema's details, to her pleasant surprise.

Sneha prattled on and on until Neema, who was listening with the same excitement, tactfully snatched a pause to interpolate, 'You must be hungry, honey. Come with me. Lemme cook something,' she said, leading Sneha to the kitchen.

Sneha hovered behind and watched Neema silently who busied herself rinsing the pan, chopping green chillies, and sautéing other ingredients. When she began to slice onions, Sneha suddenly asked leaning against the kitchen counter, 'Neema, are you okay? You seem to be thinking of something else. You have become very silent.'

Neema turned around with a start, smiled, and began to apologise, realising the quietness she had imported unwittingly.

'Sorry, honey,' she put her hand on Sneha's shoulder, opening her eyes mischievously wide. 'I was so busy cutting and chopping that I . . .' she pursed her lips and nodded, which meant *I shouldn't have done that*. Sneha's discerning smile cut her off.

'Neema, you look a bit dull.' Sneha paused, fidgeting with her fingernails while Neema resumed stirring the contents of the pan on the stove, holding onto her artificial cheerfulness.

'We have a lot to share,' Neema said after a few seconds.

'Sure baby. I have prattled enough about the street I got lost in and the people who misguided me in my effort to locate your house and the book shop I visited on my way, blah, blah, blah. Now it's time for us to speak about important things.'

She watched Neema take out the plates, cutlery, and fill the jug with water. She came forward to lend a helping hand and put them all on a tray while Neema wiped her hand and drank water directly from the huge jug. They walked into the hall with the tray and slouched on the huge, wide couch, each on one end of it, resting their backs against the cushioned armrest, facing one another with a leg propped up.

Each with a spoon dug into the hot semolina dish, they sat looking into each other's eyes, pleased to be meeting each other in their late forties after so many years.

'It'll get cold. We better eat,' said Neema.

'And talk later,' added Sneha, briskly nodding her head and snickering.

'We have a lot to share and talk. Like old times,' Neema said as she lifted the spoon to her mouth.

Sneha ate a spoonful and chuckled, 'Delicious! I've brought you something. But first, let me eat,' she said, busy relishing the contents of her plate.

Neema recalled how only at the end of eating, Sneha would hand out the gifts, unlike her other friends, who exchanged gifts before they ate.

'You are the same old person,' Neema remarked.

Their friendship had no room for misinterpretations or offence. It was a friendship that had been built upon a solid foundation of complete trust, faith, love, sympathy, and empathy. Being humble and modest were the watchwords of their friendliness. When they had finished, Sneha asked her point blank, 'Why didn't you go steady with Milan? He loved you very much, and so did you.'

'I'm regretting it now,' was Neema's pert reply. They began to giggle like the old days. Finally, Neema heaved a deep sigh and said solemnly, 'I didn't have the courage to confront my parents. It's not as if you don't know about the kind of situation I was in at my home.'

She paused and continued with a cheerful smile, 'He came to my college once, long back. We went out to my favourite icecream parlour and we caught up on old times.' She giggled and scrunched her mouth and looked into Sneha's eyes apologetically. 'I didn't make it up. Didn't call him even once. I was busy with my own life. Trying to make my marriage work.'

Sneha got a hint of Neema's feelings. She fixed her eyes on her friend and listened with a mixture of pain and regret.

'Are you happy now, anyway, with your marriage, your husband?'

Neema told her everything in retrospection and narrated in detail how everything had crumpled to dust, her trials and tribulations as a rejected wife and her great strife in bringing up her daughter single-handedly.

Sneha finally exhaled long and deep. 'Have you ever heard our society speak ill of a man? Especially of a man who does not make a good husband and is incapable of giving happiness to his wife?' she questioned vehemently with a scowl on her brow now.

'No,' Neema shook her head in the negative, sadly.

Sneha looked at her with a cynical snicker. She reached out for her bag on the centre table, pulled out a long bottle of sparkling red wine, and handed it out to Neema, 'This is for you, honey,' she said with a broad grin.

'For us,' beamed Neema with a smile, thanking her. Neema had started to relish wine, if not other alcohol. Sneha disappeared into the kitchen while Neema sat with the gift in her hand, appreciating the long, dark bottle. Sneha emerged, eagerly uncorked it, poured it into two big goblets, and handed one to her friend with a beaming smile. They raised it in a toast, clicked their glasses, and settled down again to pour out their lives' stuff.

Sniffing the wine, Sneha said, 'I never got married. Know why?'

'Why?' Neema smacked the sweet liquor on her lips and looked at her curiously. Raising the goblet to the level of her eyes, Sneha said with a smirk, 'The guy with whom my romance was going steady demanded a huge dowry.' She paused. Neema saw the pain it had brought back on her friend's face. Sneha continued, 'My parents had retired. My dad had spent much of his money on his brothers and sisters. We didn't have much left to acquiesce to all of the demands this guy's sister placed on our cards.' She placed the goblet on the table, pulled out a tissue from her purse, and looked at Neema, clearing her nose. 'I rejected him outright. My poor parents wanted to sell the only house we had and move to a little rented house just to see me happily married. Do you think I would have been happy? With a bastard like him?'

A hint of a smile broke on Neema's lips, although she could see the anguish in her friend's tone and the pain, insult, and humiliation she had gone through. The smile that had broken on her face was simply because her friend had referred to the man as a bastard.

Neema turned her head towards the window in a reflective mood. The sharp evening rays were beating down. There was a brief silence until the doorbell broke their contemplative thoughts. Neema rushed to open the door, knowing that Goldie was back from college, and Sneha followed closely on her heels. Goldie was excited to have a guest at home. She flashed a sweet, benign smile when Sneha was introduced.

'Taller than your mom,' Sneha remarked appreciatively. She turned to Neema and said, 'Your daughter is very pretty.'

Goldie was all smiles and pleased with the flattery. There was hardly anyone who visited them except for her own friends occasionally. She went to her room to wash up and was back downstairs within minutes. For the first time, there was a guest at home her mom was happy to have, and Goldie was happy for her. Neema could see the warm smile on her girl's face. Only once Goldie had the opportunity in one of her friends' house to sit among adults and listen with pleasure and a laid back contentment to their old-time tales that evoked an old world charm. She was pleased when Sneha gave her a huge hug, led her by the hand to the couch, and divulged how she and Neema had enjoyed their college days. Meanwhile, Neema disappeared into the kitchen to cook dinner.

Goldie kept running her long fingers through her shiny, silky long black hair and listened interestedly, all smiles. A few minutes later, when she went to the kitchen for a glass of water, she whispered excitedly into her mom's ears, 'Mama, your friend put her arms around me and told me to call her 'aunty,' and Neema knew that this warmth and affection from someone who infused a sense of belongingness was something Goldie had missed all her life. She had met her mom's own sister, Mili, only once in her life and had encountered nothing more than an awkward smile and a stiff hello and a little bit of criticism for having worn a short dress.

As soon as Neema joined them in the living room, Goldie asked her mother hesitantly, 'Is aunty going to stay with us tonight?'

It was past eight and Sneha had not showed any signs of leaving.

'Of course she will,' replied Neema, throwing an unsure glance at her friend, who quietly smiled at Goldie.

After dinner, relaxing in the cool, breezy balcony upstairs, Sneha narrated interesting, funny anecdotes and time flew by. The air was filled with fun and laughter that was so unusual from their otherwise drab evenings. It was past midnight when the trio walked downstairs noisily, for there was no one else in the house to silence them.

The girls dropped down and curled up on the queen-size bed. For the first time Goldie who slept between the two, felt safe, secure, loved, and befriended. Neema could see it from her happy countenance. Her child had never laughed so much in a carefree manner all her life. *There still exists a world that can bring with it countable pleasures,* she reflected, lying supine. Goldie was breathing full and easy as she gradually slipped to deep slumber blanketed by sheer happiness.

Chapter Twenty-Four

After Goldie left for school the next morning, Neema and Sneha settled happily on the couch in the living room, each with a cup of coffee, and resumed their intimate conversation. As Sneha spoke, Neema listened, silently, like a child. 'The fact that you have not revolted nor fought for your place as his legal wife, nor made any effort to investigate the reason behind his truancy has now left you at the rope's end,' Sneha said with a note of pity in her tone. 'You feel defeated. I can see that from your emaciated face. Darling, you had so much energy. You were vivacious. It was you who inspired and led all the girls on the campus to throw out that professor who had beaten his wife. What happened to your rebellious spirit?'

'When you become alone,' Neema answered reflectively, 'you become helpless. It is only with age you start growing tougher and of course, a little support has to come your way, you see. Women themselves speak ill of other women. To whom can you turn to for help, Sneha?'

'A woman who adds fuel to the embers left behind by a man does not realise that she is only becoming a slave to him. It's her foolishness,' Sneha remarked and continued after a brief silence, 'Don't you think women are snobbish? I once went on a tour with a women's group and a south Indian lady I met, who claimed to be a doctor and spoke of her plans to work for charity organisations, chose to become friends only with some of the stylish north Indians and was highly prejudiced towards the others. That's the irony. Imagine the kind of relation she might have with her patients?' She shrugged in exasperation.

'There are also women,' she continued, 'who listen to your sad story for a while and quickly add, "I have only a few minutes to spare. My husband and children will return anytime, and I have to attend to them." These mundane creatures expect you to spew in crystal form a lifetime of emotions you have suffered, as if you have been in a game of cricket. Listening to your woes is like a 'time pass' game for them so that they have something to gossip later, which is another time pass. They don't care a shit for the reeking life you are suffering with. Ironically, they might even stop smiling at you later like you are a castaway because you are not like the rest with a secure family. Ultimately, what good has it done to you when the listener does not have the patience to feel the pain of your emotions! What good it is to share your problems with such people? You might as well sit before God and cry your heart out. The Lord of the Heaven will not make you feel guilty for having spoken out plaintively. She took a sip of water and continued, 'Know something? I had a colleague, who I mistook to be a good friend, as we had known each other for a long time and so ventured to share some of my concerns and problems with her. That was a time when I needed someone to care for me, give me some love, who would ask me if I needed any help, but here I had a friend who in the end got up saying, "Very sorry. Take care."'

Neema was gravely listening with her eyes bent down, her forefinger running back and forth on the tip of her thumb nail. She felt the pain her friend had gone through. She finally lifted her eyes and looked into Sneha's with despondency.

Sneha, who bounced back to her cheerful self, finally pronounced a resolution. 'You must make friends with Milan again, dear. You have a right to live your life, no matter what society thinks of you.'

'No,' Neema said quickly and firmly. 'My daughter is nineteen and I don't want to drive wrong notions into her head and soil her moral behaviour.'

Sneha was at a loss for words. She quietly looked at Neema's face while the latter looked away into nothingness through the window, conspicuously reflecting over things before she turned her head nimbly and avowed pleasantly with a smile, 'I'm perfectly used to living in my own world of fantasy. There is one person I love, however, and Goldie takes it as a jest.'

'Who is that?' Sneha asked with a twinkle in her eyes.

'Bobby Deol, the film actor,' announced Neema.

Sneha threw up her head and screamed with laughter at Neema's preposterous answer. 'I'm amused. Amused with what you say.' She pulled out a tissue and cleared her running nose. 'Are you serious?' she queried, laughing furiously, rubbing the tears off her eyes.

'I didn't say I'm in love,' Neema added. 'I only said that I love him because he has given me the strength to live.'

Half-smiling and half-serious, she got up as if to prepare more coffee to avoid further discussion on it, for she was aware of the inanity of such a fancy, also she being an aged woman, supposed to be mature in outlook.

Sneha stood up too and followed her into the kitchen, snickering, 'It is this childlike quality of yours I've always liked in you, Neema. Many people don't understand you. But I do. Your friends do, and Milan does. It is precisely this which has helped you overcome the tough phases of your life. Through your tears, you are always drawn into the little pleasantries of nature that keeps you happy like a child. You are such a sweet darling.'

Neema scrunched her lips with a smile as she started to cut the vegetables, but she had sobered up and Sneha was sensitive enough to detect it. Finally leaning against the counter, Sneha said, '"Procreativity" or "Libido," which means sexual urge, according to the Father of Psycho-analysis, Sigmund Freud, has been the motive force for all human activity. Tell me, Neema, don't you have a fire burning in you?'

'I have my own way to allay it,' Neema snickered.

Sneha tilted her head to the side and struck her palm to her forehead lightly.

Neema giggled into her knuckles. 'No fear of STD,' she said and turned her head towards her friend.

Sneha finally fell into a hearty giggle.

Neema maintained her propriety without giggling, this time to substantiate her statement. 'Look, honey,' she said at length, 'I have a grown-up daughter. I have to protect her. I can't trust any man, you know. Moreover, let me tell you. This maybe a cosmopolitan city, but people suffer from exotropia even if a brother visits a lonely woman.'

Sneha gave out a loud laugh. 'You have used the right term.' She went on laughing. She swooped and put her arms around Neema's neck, and could utter no more than, 'Oh, Neema.'

She had suffered too. After her traumatic break, she hadn't had the courage to trust any man.

They set plates on the dining table and sat for their lunch. It was now Neema who started to prattle.

'When a single woman is all smiles, our society jumps to the conclusion that she must be enjoying, otherwise she wouldn't have had the guts to go out with lipstick and a smile. What they don't realise is that she has become a walking zombie, dead in spirit, yet fighting to live like a normal person.' A long silence fell as they ate and relished the food.

'Our men and women,' said Neema after they had washed their hands and cleared the table, 'who ardently worship our gods and goddesses, have not learnt to respect women or their thoughts. Our female gods have exhibited unspeakable strength, power, and valour in our spiritual literature. It's a shame on our men to disrespect or disregard a woman's dignity, her emotional needs and her stand in society. Have you heard the story of Bahucara Devi?' she continued. 'As a beautiful goddess, she is deceived into a false marriage with a homosexual man who neglects her in pursuit of other men. She follows him one day and finds him sporting in a stream with other young men. She asks, "If you were like this, why did you marry me and ruin my life?" He replies that he was forced into marriage so that he could father children and continue the family line. Infuriated, she castrates him and declares: "Men like you (who dishonestly marry women) should instead emasculate themselves and dress as women. From now on, even you men will worship me as a goddess!"In another instance, she is forced to cut off her breasts to avoid being raped by an evil man. As she bleeds to death, she curses him to become impotent.' A brief silence fell as the two needed time to gulp the rage that had erupted in them.

'That is very interesting. I didn't know these stories,' remarked Sneha after a while.

Neema continued in a motivated spirit, 'One time, Kali was engaged in a universal war so fierce that her fury went out of control. All the gods were terrified and no one could end her ruthless slaughter. They approached Lord Siva as a last resort and Siva, not sure what to do, prostrated before the goddess in full surrender to her power.'

'Exactly,' Sneha cut in, 'a woman can be very powerful, Neema. Get up and freshen up. When Goldie comes home, we are going out to have some fun. It's half past three.'

Neema hopped up jubilantly.

Sneha had proved her resilient friendship that had developed so many years ago. Their friendship had survived and Neema was very thankful to God for bringing Sneha back into her life again. She was such a source of strength, an independent entrepreneur who had her own plant nursery business. Neema adored her all the more now for her efforts in helping Neema bounce back to a joyful, fuller life despite her own disappointed lonely life.

CHAPTER TWENTY-FIVE

Babu took the afternoon bus to Madikeri. His sole mission was to bring back Arjun from the clutches of Priya and save Neema's marriage, if possible. His desire to experience the big city suddenly had become insignificant to him. He had chalked out a plan and wanted to pursue it single-mindedly.

It was unbearably chilly and almost dark by the time he arrived in Madikeri. In spite of his woollen sweater and muffler, he found himself freezing and his fingers numb. By the time he walked about a kilometre uphill with his briefcase to a decent, modest hotel in the vicinity of the busstand, he was panting for breath with parched lips.

He had planned out his moves and accordingly, he telephoned Shravana, when it was half past eleven, knowing fully well that the so-called boss would have returned from work. He said he called to say that he had reached Hassan absolutely safe. Babu further thanked him for the wonderful stay he had with him, bid him good night, and hung up the phone relieved, for no suspicion could be traced in his boss' voice.

After a sumptuous breakfast and coffee the next morning, Babu approached the front desk and enquired with the receptionist whether she knew the wealthy landlord, Dasappa. In a small town like Madikeri, Babu knew pretty well that almost everyone knew everybody who was a permanent resident there, except for the very insignificant. He had conjectured that talking with Priya's father would be the practical first step to dissuade the woman from continuing with Arjun. His premise was that Dasappa, being a wealthy landlord, would be a respectable, aged man and definitely would not want his only daughter to fall into the web of a married man. The young, fair, plump, cheerful receptionist clad in a white floral silk sari and tomato red woollen sweater turned to Babu. 'Oh! The baron of Madikeri, Dasappa!' she sighed with a chuckle.

'There is a doctor on Gandhi's street. It's best for you to meet him, sir. He will be able to tell you much about Dasappa,' she replied politely.

'Can you please give me the doctor's address?'

She scribbled it on a piece of paper and handed it over to him.

'Kiran clinic, Gandhi Street,' she smiled and got back to work attending other customers.

Babu thanked her and wasted no time in starting off on his investigation. He wrapped the muffler around his head and headed towards Gandhi Street. He had walked for over half a kilometre on steep ascents and descents before he halted and enquired a passer-by. The stranger pointed it out below. It was almost a kilometre down a spiral terrain that weaved its path through acres of thick plantation. The clinic was a modest cottage with a fresh coat of white paint and gabled roof of Mangalore red tiles standing forlorn in the middle of a peaceful glade.

With his hands in his pockets, Babu began descending the, narrow, winding lanealong the stretch of an old compound wall to his left. On his right was a stretch of brush and bush with hedgehogs and beggar lice, a vast stretch as far as the eye could see that prompted Babu to dream of becoming a landowner someday. Halfway down the road, he saw a half-open rickety bamboo gate in the compound wall. He pushed it open and stepped inside apprehensively. Except for the sound of crickets, there was no other sound in the silent air.

Babu walked into the clearing and took in the sylvan surroundings with a deep, long breath and saw, fifty metres away, a couple putting on their slippers near the door of the clinic. Tension weighed on him, thinking of the kind of encounter he might have with this doctor. He had come there on personal work and not as a patient.

Would this doctor concede to talk personal things in the first place? Would he help me meet Dasappa? If I do meet the landowner, would he be able to influence Dasappa to dissuade his daughter, Priya, from hooking onto a married man who had an innocent and beautiful wife? In the first place, what kind of person would Dasappa be? What if Arjun came to know that I had cheated him, violating the principles of servility and integrity for which I and my mother are known for? Have I unnecessarily meddled in Arjun's personal affairs?

Brooding over these thoughts, Babu walked slowly first and finally pushing aside his thoughts;he walked the distance decisively towards the clinic. The couple had left and there was heavy silence everywhere. He loitered for a few seconds outside, took a deep breath, and, with his hands still in his pockets, made a short mental prayer and ducked in with a plastic smile.

Babu shook hands with the doctor and said confidently that he was from Bangalore and that he had come there to buy a piece of land that belonged to Mr Dasappa. In that connection, he said, he was making enquiries as to Dasappa's integrity in business dealings and that the receptionist of a certain hotel in the town had referred the doctor to him, that being the purpose of his visit.

The doctor, Kiran, now in his forties, tall, hefty, a decent-looking gentleman with a receding hairline gave a conceding smile and motioned to the chair opposite him. Babu sat across him and was immediately put at ease, but when the doctor said, 'So, you want to buy Dasappa's property? You know nothing about this Dasappa?' Babu's tension crept back, for a second till he consciously fought to regain his composure by hastily gulping down the glass of cold water the doctor had kept for himself on the table. *Was he about to hear something shocking about Dasappa?*

'I only know that he owns a lot of land and that he is interested in selling an acre or so. The only other thing I know about this Dasappa is that he has a daughter by name Priya who is an advocate in Bangalore,' answered Babu nonchalantly and waited for the doctor to speak.

'Advocate?' the doctor shot towards Babu with a sneer. 'I don't think she even passed her law exam.'

Babu observed a sudden disturbed look on the doctor's face. The man had now shifted his glance towards his folded hands on the table. After a while, he shook his head agitatedly. 'He is a murderer. Dasappa. You have to tread carefully.'

Babu froze for a second, while the doctor recomposed himself. Nevertheless, quickly and astutely, Babu composed himself too and cleared his throat.

That girl Priya who he had seen on Arjun's lap was the daughter of a murderer? Having recovered himself, he nodded in disbelief, almost innocently. *How on earth had Arjun got associated with such people?*

He looked down and swirled the round pink glass paperweight on the glass-topped mahogany table to avoid looking at the doctor, lest his flustered looks betrayed the thoughts that were running in his mind. He heaved a pathetic sigh and asked the doctor almost innocently, if he knew anything about Dasappa's daughter, Priya.

It was a long time since Kiran had any visitors with whom he could at leisure prattle a little about those bygone days. He told Babu everything about Priya at a slow pace, in a relaxed disposition, and even got Babu a cup of coffee from a nearby hotel.

What he heard thoroughly shook Babu out of his wits. He got up, thanking the doctor for having warned him in his business dealing. The doctor got up too. He shook hands and further added, 'The property is not even legitimate. He got it transferred to his name after murdering his younger brother with the help of one Mr Arjun, a lawyer in Bangalore.' Babu's ears and visage went red as he trembled within. Shock and fear invaded him, hiking up his blood pressure. He thanked the doctor once again and left.

He walked out into the chill grey day with his hands in his pockets, brooding over what he had just heard. Things seemed to fall into place. The bastard had both Dasappa's money and his daughter to enjoy. Whether he had been an accomplice or not to the murder, certainly he had applied his legal shrewdness to cover up things. Murder, sex, liquor, drag—he had reached the realm of the damned! He had cheated a poor soul. Neema's pretty face and her sweet, innocent voice invaded Babu's thoughts. He resolved to meet Kanthi and let her know the dark secret he had just unearthed.

When he got into the bus that evening to get back to Bangalore, he did not surrender to sleep. His mind worked, worked from all angles as to how best he could help Neema. 'Tread carefully.' He reflected on the doctor's words before he gave in to the dull, monotonous motion of the bus and dozed off, the cold wind blowing against his face through the half-open window.

CHAPTER TWENTY-SIX

In a big city like Bangalore, his short-time boss, Shravana certainly wouldn't know that he was in town.

With this thought, Babu checked into a suburban hotel that night but didn't go straight to bed after dinner, for there were things to think and unanswered questions knocking at his temples. He telephoned his mother and asked her whether she had heard anything from Arjun or Shravana.

She replied in the negative, her tone betraying her feeling of sudden doubt about her son's affairs in the metropolitan city.

'Are you safe?' She anxiously tried to prod into the matter

'Nothing is the matter, Ma. I was just curious to know about it. I'll call you again in a few days. Take care,' said Babu and hung up the phone.

He sat in the in the dull, little room on the third floor of the budget hotel smoking and thinking. He conjured Arjun's face and the look in his eyes. They had a glassy twinkle—a pair of light green balls floating in the whites like cat's eyes. He saw villainy and cunningness in them as he exhaled the smoke through his thinly parted lips. He recalled Arjun's visage over and over again and slowly became aware of the falsity of the person. Shrewd! He was indeed utterly shrewd!

Babu went to the dark little balcony overlooking the avenue of trees and flung his cigarette butt into the dark wilderness in a rage. Standing there, he watched the dark sky and pulled out another cigarette. This time, he threw the butt onto the mosaic floor of the balcony and crushed it with his hawai slippers. *The daredevil bimbo had ensnared Arjun! Who did she live with in Bangalore?* He loped in angrily and flopped onto the spring bed, determined to find out more about that daredevil, Priya, and decided to locate her place of residence first.

The next day, in a black pullover, the hood pulled over his head, he hung outside the premises of the civil court, keeping an eye out for Priya. He had hired a motorbike to follow her. When he couldn't spot her even after twelve noon, he started questioning some lady lawyers about her. It was only when he referred to Arjun and said that she was Arjun's secretary that he succeeded in getting her residential address.

He started off on his hired motor bike around two in the afternoon. He turned into a lane in Shanthinagar. The search was rather difficult. The ascendency of the numbers on the houses was rather confusing. However, one house in the middle of a row of houses bore the number he was looking for. Its doors were closed and the metal lattice window betrayed no life of its occupants. He lowered the stand of his bike and nervously pushed the metal gate. A wooden plate on the door of the mediocre house read Priya Hanumanthappa, B.Sc., LLB, advocate. If Priya opened the door, he would tell her that it was out of sheer serendipity that he had reached there, as he had come to the area in search of a friend. With this resolution, he held his breath tight and pressed the button on the outer jamb firmly.

A woman in her sixties, clad in a cotton sari, opened the door.

'Yes?' she said with a puzzled look.

'Is lawyer Priya home?' he asked nervously.

'No, Come on in.' the woman ushered him in. 'You had any work with madam?' she asked politely.

'I'm Mr Santosh, practicing lawyer. I wanted to talk to Miss Priya regarding some urgent matter,' he said brazenly now that she was not at home.

'Mrs Priya,' she corrected him cheerfully. 'Well, she is not at home right now. Can I take a message for her?' she asked.

'She lives here alone?' Babu queried.

'Oh, no,' she laughed. 'Her husband is here. He doesn't keep well. He is regularly on injections.'

'O, I'm so sorry. What is wrong with him? I mean . . .' he quickly added, 'not my business. But I'm really sorry for madam.'

'I don't know what he is suffering from,' replied the maid. 'I only give him the shots I'm instructed with and trained in, er, you know, trained by madam herself,' she said. 'You want to meet the professor? Poor man! His illness binds him to the bed much of the time. Does madam know you were coming?'

'Well, not really. A matter came up urgently and I thought of hopping in. That's okay. Thank you very much.' He turned to leave.

'In fact, most of the days, she stays in a ladies hostel in Jayanagar. If it's urgent, probably you can meet her up there,' the maid said. 'She has not been attending court for the past one week because of other commitments. If you really want to meet her, it is better you telephone her before you goto make sure she is available.'

Babu smiled diffidently while she handed him a chit with the hostel's telephone number on it. He thanked and left, letting the victorious feeling catch his breath as the cool evening wind hit his face. He stopped on the way and put on his helmet. *She is married?* That was news to him. *Yet, she stays in a hostel!* That was confusing to Babu.

Doctor Kiran had told him everything, but hadn't seemed to know that she was wedded to the professor.

Babu's next destination was a long drive of over an hour amidst the crowded traffic. He spat thrice at the third traffic signal in wrath and disgust at the way things were revealing and burgeoning in a slow progress. Confused thoughts crowded his mind. *Help me think later!* He screamed to his mind as he undulated through the evening flow of vehicles. It wasn't an easy task locating a working women's hostel in the anfractuous residential area. Finally, there among a row of posh houses, he saw a big brown wooden board that read *women's hostel* painted in bold white letters over the front of the building. He pulled his bike suddenly, glanced at the wide open door, and caught sight of a woman behind the receptionist desk. Feeling a bit nervous, he took his time shutting off the engine and wondered whether he should go inside or turn back and give it up. The woman behind the receptionist desk was staring at him from inside.

'You are looking out for someone here in the hostel?' she asked.

Babu, who had stationed himself right in front of the gate without the least expectation of being questioned, was taken aback by this sudden confrontation that didn't allow him to mask his words. He hadn't observed her coming out. He had not even rehearsed his words.

'Er, I was looking for Priya, lawyer Priya,' he blurted out.

'With so many crimes against women on the rise, we do not encourage men visitors in this hostel,' she said sternly and asked, 'Is Priya your girlfriend?'

'No! No, my colleague. Actually, my cousin.'

'Haven't you informed her of your visit? She left with her husband to Madikeri a week ago.' The warden adjusted her spectacles.

'O, her husband, Arjun?' His heart leapt with a melange of feelings—anxiety, curiosity, fears, all at once.

'Yes. The poor girl stays in this hostel, as her husband works in a different town,' she said with apathy.

'When is she returning?' he asked.

'I don't know, sir.' She looked away from him, exasperated. 'Leave your card, if you have one, so I can give it to her when she returns,' she said and turned her back on him.

Babu fidgeted in his pockets and pretended to have forgotten it. She turned again and asked, 'Your name?'

'Santhosh. I'm a lawyer too,' he said, straddling his motorbike. As soon as he had said it, he knew that he had committed an irrevocable blunder. Glancing at the warden's back, he hit the gas tank of his bike with his fist and spit the word 'shit' with anger.

Arjun would certainly know that no lawyer by name Santhosh would come to the hostel looking for Priya, and Priya would definitely probe into the semblance of such a fib as having a cousin by name Santhosh.

He buckled his helmet and kicked the starter of his bike furiously.

CHAPTER TWENTY-SEVEN

Arjun and Priya had returned in the wee hours of that morning from their foreign bash—an expensive trip to Hong Kong for about a week. Now back in Bangalore, they checked into a five-star hotel somewhere on old Airport Road, as they wished to relax in privacy.

In the luxury hotel, far removed from the hustle and bustle of the suburbs, almost on the outskirts of Bangalore, Arjun and Priya, in their elegantly embellished room, got engrossed in making love. They were hungrier for their physical bodies than they were for breakfast. They emptied two whiskeys and were on a high. It was almost twelve noon when they went in for a shower.

Sitting by the window in a bikini, her hair still damp, Priya munched toast with a blank mind while Arjun sat opposite her in a white bathrobe, sipping coffee contentedly and pleased with all the good things that were happening to him.

Dasappa had accepted him as his son-in-law and heir to his property, running to crores of rupees. It was time that he did something to oust Neema before she or his daughter could claim some of his property. Oust Neema! With a lopsided smile and glint in his moist eyes, he bent his head and looked at the last dreg of coffee in the cup.

Kanthi had entrusted him with a legal task, and he had half-finished it. He remembered it now. He had gone through the value of the property. He would soon have to make a will on behalf of Kanthi, which would make her second daughter, Mili, rich. Paradoxical! The first daughter not getting anything! A corner of his mouth gave in to an ironical smile. He lifted up his eyebrows in deep thought. He had to be scrupulous in typing out the other document, which would make Kanthi liable to pay him a minimum of fifty lakhs by way of acknowledging his legal service to her.

Priya kicked his knee with her foot and brought him back to the present. They started to laugh and decided to stay confined to their presidential suite the entire day, enjoying the luxury of in-room services.

Sometime in the twilight hours, Priya telephoned home casually. The maid told her that a young lawyer had come by looking for her, saying that an urgent legal matter had come up which had necessitated his visit and that being the matter, the maid had been prompted to give him Priya's hostel address.

Upset and angry with the maid for having foolishly given an unknown person her hostel address, she made enquiries about her sick husband rather indignantly and asked roughly, 'Did you give the old man his injection? Tell him I'm held up with my work and will not be free for another few days.' She didn't wait to hear a 'yes' from the maid. She hung up the phone in a huff. The drug, fentanyl, was working wonders. She wished for the old professor's quick death.

Next, when she telephoned the hostel, the warden broke the news about the young man's visit. 'He said he was a lawyer and your cousin,' she said cheerfully.

Priya, who did not have any male cousin, in the first place, was distraught to hear it. Moreover, no male lawyer ever dared visit her in the hostel. As far as she knew, none in the legal fraternity knew about her association with a hostel. Everyone knew she worked with Arjun and legal matters were discussed with him, he being her boss. Arjun was alarmed when she told him about the young man.

After dinner, sipping coffee in the silent, dimly lit round-the-clock bamboo coffee shop, an annexure of the five-star hotel, they discussed the issue with sobriety. Who on earth could be the intruder? Who the hell was it that had started to spy on her?

'Your wife could have sent someone,' she said with a note of edginess. 'Call her. Do something,' she insisted. 'Find out who the hell it is and what the fuck is going on!'

They ordered another pot of coffee; although it was nigh on quarter to twelve. They began to reconnoitre and counted a few names they could think of as suspects. Somehow, none of them seemed to match the description as given by the maid and the warden. Arjun's mind worked briskly. Babu had left the very next day after he had seen him in the most obscene situation with Priya.

He took out his mobile from his shirt pocket and punched Babu's numbers.

The long ring went futile. Arjun disconnected it and telephoned again with indignation. After a long ring, to his relief, Babu answered the call.

'How are you? I'm coming to Hassan tomorrow,' said Arjun, winking at Priya, who was sitting opposite him in the darker corner, staring at him ebulliently.

'Are you there?' Arjun called, flummoxed over Babu's abrupt silence. 'Where are you, by the way?' he asked, deliberately, trying his best to sound casual.

Babu, daunted, blurted unconsciously, 'Gulmuhar Paradise.'

He, who was relaxing after dinner, had not expected any call from anybody that late in the night. With a cigarette between his fingers, he was in fact planning his intended visit to Neema's house in the morning.

He was gripped with apprehension, when he saw that it was Arjun's call and was unprepared to answer the questions he might receive.

Now that he had he been discovered, an ache shot through his head. Arjun had played his game and had hung the phone abruptly. 'Hello, Babu squeaked once again, 'hello,' enervated.

Patting the sweat on his brow, he unbuttoned his white mull kurta, turned the fan on full blast, ordered for some tea and utterly consternated, pulled out another cigarette and checked the time on his mobile. It was half past twelve, midnight.

What if Arjun called his mother, who was oblivious of her son's pursuit and the fact that he had quit his job? He checked the time once again. Could he get a bus to Hassan at that time of the night? And if he left immediately, he would never be able to apprise Neema of the discoveries that he had made. He would also never get a chance to occlude Priya's affair with Arjun. There were still things for him to do. His final resolution was to rush through things before Arjun could ascertain anything. He jumped into bed and rolled restlessly until the break of dawn.

At five, he leapt up to telephone Neema.

'Hello,' a mellifluous voice said on the other end.

'I'm Babu, didi. Sorry to be bothering you at this odd time,' he said gently fighting hard to mask the rising anxiety in his voice.

'No problem at all,' she said sweetly. 'Is anything the matter, Babu?'

'Er, nothing serious. I'm still in Bangalore. I wasn't able to sleep. I have a few things to tell you, didi, before I leave for Hassan. If you will permit me to come home, I would like to meet you around nine.'

'You are most welcome, Babu,' she told him kindly and cheerfully and also told him that her mother, who was his mom's best friend, was in the hospital. She gave him the hospital's address so that he could visit her, if he wanted to.

CHAPTER TWENTY-EIGHT

Arjun looked at Priya with a glint in his eyes, elated about his discovery and of having fixed the suspect and shared with her his next plan of action.

The two left the coffee house at quarter to one and reached their suite, ambling through the vast stretch of the hotel's lovely garden. Arjun dropped himself on the bed exhausted, but kept sleep at stake for he had a plan of action which he had to execute before things ran out of hand. He was determined to pin down Babu. *Was he by any chance in communication with Neema? He had to ferret it out.*

It was barely dawn when he jolted out of slumber. He had seen a bad dream. He sat in bed and looked around. Priya's wristwatch, with its heart-shaped dial on its gold chain, showed that it was already half past four. He slipped out of bed, got into the shower, and dressed quickly. He carefully picked up the shirt that had no perfume spoor, slipped the tiny, wireless video camera which he had bought in Hong Kong, into his trouser pocket, and stealthily slipped out of the room. Priya wasn't disturbed. She was fast asleep. As he drove home in the still darkness of the rising dawn, his mind raced to figure out the strategies he would expedite.

He turned the key softly and with his socked feet noiselessly climbed the stairs in his huge house illuminated by the single corner lamp. Both Goldie's door as well as Neema's was closed. Leaning against the elliptic railing of the upper hall, he unscrewed the small plastic plate that concealed the round, black hole of the ceiling light, took out the tiny instrument from his pocket, placed it securely inside the socket, and screwed back the concealer. Hastily, he scrambled down the stairs and was back inside his car. Within moments, he was driving back to the hotel, while Babu was hanging up the phone after his brief conversation with Neema.

It was quarter to eight when Babu left the hotel. The sun's soft rays shone bright and cheerful when he headed to the hospital to visit Kanthi.

Seeing her effete and paralysed, he held back from disclosing the information he had dug up and checked himself from telling or asking her anything that was on his mind. He sat on her bed gloomily, holding her hand and stroking her head with affection and assurance. She merely looked at him, unable to talk. He carefully placed the fruits and flowers he had brought with him on the metal side table and left hurriedly.

The sun was already strong at quarter past nine when Babu reached Neema's house. Neema had already briefed her friend Sneha about the visitor and fondly remembered the lovely time she had spent with Babu and his mother.

Babu's blush of shyness became obvious, when Neema put her hand on his shoulder to usher him into the hall. After pleasantries, Neema excused herself and disappeared into the kitchen leaving Sneha and him to chat. Within no time, Neema was back with a tray of fruits, cookies and a pot of coffee.

She saw that he was too eager to inform her of what he had seen and unearthed.

'It's something about Arjun, didi.' He paused to study Neema's reaction. 'I have discovered a few things, which I want to speak about.'

Neema glanced at Sneha and an impassive communication of understanding passed between the two in their exchanged looks.

'Go on. We don't mind listening to what you have discovered about her husband. He is involved in an extra-marital affair. Isn't he?' Sneha said nonchalantly.

'Yes, didi.' There was a kind of hesitation and guilt in his large, innocent-looking boyish eyes. Neema looked at him with a smile. 'Go on,' she said gently.

He narrated everything that he had raked up on his trip to Madikeri and everything that he had seen and experienced in the dingy apartment.

In the end, there were tears in Neema's eyes. Sneha disappeared into the kitchen and came back with another pot of coffee. Neema was smiling again. After all, she was born under a star that always helped her bounce back to her normal self quickly once her emotion had found its vent. That was nature's gift for her—a blessing or curse in disguise, she often wondered. And all the people always thought that she was always happy and cheerful—a miracle! They envied her for it.

Babu didn't stay for lunch, although the girls forced him to. *What if Arjun was already on his way to Hassan? Or what if his shrewd senses had taken him to Gulmohar Paradise?*

When he got up to leave, the impulse to plant a kiss on Neema's cheek so overpowered him that he fixed his eyes on her with an overflowing current of pity and love.

'Thanks for everything, Babu,' she said with genuine kindness, stepped forward and gave him a gentle hug. 'You have taken all this trouble for my sake.' But he wasn't listening. He was trying to fight the dizziness of pleasure that had engulfed him. He held her in his arms lightly and went weak in his limbs. His eyes, which looked deep into hers, were filled with passion and pathos, making it explicit that he was fond of her. There wasn't a smile on his lips, but his large, black, emotional eyes told it all.

Sneha held out a scribbling pad and a pen in front of Babu and requested he give Priya's residential as well as her hostel address, which he quickly and readily scribbled and then hurriedly took his leave. When he reached the door with the girls following him, he turned and said, 'Neema didi, please save my phone number. You can call me anytime for any help. I'm always there for you.'

The apparition of her benign smiling face, so pretty and charming, went with him when he boarded the bus to

Hassan around one o'clock in the afternoon after a quick luncheon in the bus stand canteen.

He took the window seat and settled in the red government bus. An uneasy fear lurked in him. As the bus drove out of Bangalore into the windy outskirts, he felt much lighter for having disengaged himself finally from the vortex of danger and deceit and happily snoozed off in the cold breeze that was blowing from the window of the racing bus.

Arjun, having returned to the suite hurried Priya to pack up. They drove straight to Shravana's bachelor room to set up the computer screen so that it caught the signals of the remote camera he had fixed up in his house.

After Shravana left for his office, Arjun and Priya sat and watched curiously the happenings at his home.

Babu had found out all. *The minion had dared to do it.* A trusted, old-time neighbour, whose mother was in a servile position once and had even worked in his own house and had eaten their food! A feeling of hatred for Babu shot through Arjun. Could this have been the way to return his loyalty for having brought him to Bangalore? He threw the pillow on the floor and paced the room in rage, hitting his fist into his other palm.

He suddenly knew what he had to do next. He shared his thoughts with Priya and spent the rest of the day preparing legal documents, as he knew that he could meet the astrologer-cum-black magician only the next day, as there would be a heavy rush of people with him as evening drew on.

When he hit the bed, he couldn't wait for dawn to broach. He was restless and perturbed. Earnest revenge was the feeling that surged in him. He sat up again and sipped beer with fish fries and chicken biryani at midnight, which they had ordered from their favourite nearby restaurant. He turned and looked at Shravana and Tara, who were fast asleep without a worry.

Arjun sneaked out from the warm bachelor room, early in the morning, wearing a pair of casual trousers and a sweater. The streets were still dark and chill with lone street dogs blankly staring into nothingness. As he drove through unknown lanes, he saw lone beggars holding on to their doled-out black mantles, plodding through the deserted streets and scheming with parched lips and dirty, wide eyes in the wintry chill of early January.

He drove through the narrow cobbled lanes of the unknown area with hovels on either side, where men were brushing and spitting in the gullies of filthy water that lazed its unknown course under the intermittentgranite slabsthat bridged the front of their abodes with the dusty road. Some women were already washing clothes or dishes in front of their little houses with stored buckets of water. Arjun scanned the address again as he drove. This astrologer who appeared regularly in the ad columns of daily newspapers had visited his office in Gandhi bazaar many years ago to promote himself and had promised help when needed. He had claimed that even politicians and other celebrities sought his help in achieving their

He pulled his car in front of the little house and knocked on the door with a mild degree of anxiety gnawing somewhere deep inside him. The small double doors of the little window in the wall some three feet away from the main door were open, but everything looked dark from outside. There were a few herbal plants in the little frontyard. The astrologer, clad in a black lungi and a light-coloured checkered shirt, opened the door and ushered him in and led him into the small room that had the little window.

Usually people started visiting him only from around ten o'clock, and it was a bit strange that this guest who introduced himself as Arjun had come so early. The astrologer glanced at the little clock on the wall and saw that it was just twenty minutes past eight. He wore his glasses and stealthily took another look at Arjun from the top of the rim, guessing from his experience that the matter could be of a grave nature. He also inferred that Arjun would not be short of financial resources to get his objective executed.

Having been a black magician for years, he was no less skilful in assessing people from their outward look. He switched on the tube light, pulled out his almanacs and a few cowries, and got ready for discussion. Arjun pulled out a passport-sized photo of Babu from his pants pocket and put it on the table. While the astrologer scrutinised the photo of Babu, Arjun waited tensely studying the astrologer's thick cushion of black beard, his coarse black hair tied behind in a knot, three horizontal lines of holy ash drawn on his forehead, and the bunch of incense sticks that glowed on a corner stool in front of Gods' pictures behind the astrologer, filling the room with its flowery fragrance.

'Yes, what you want me to do?' the astrologer asked, scratching his left elbow. His huge silver ring, with nine precious gems in it, glistened in the shaft of sunlight that was now beginning to fall on the velvet cloth covering the top of the wooden table.

'I want this person dead before the end of the day,' said Arjun.

He caught the unsure look on the astrologer's face, though the man's head was still bent toward the picture.

'I mean it,' Arjun said gravely. 'He is not the great, good guy that I had thought him to be. Before he can spread stories about me in my native town, Hassan, to malign my name, I want him dead.'

Though the astrologer had the hunch to dissuade Arjun from doing such a thing to a young man, who he guessed could be a good-hearted commoner, he found himself unable to say anything, for Arjun's firm voice was rather decisive.

'It will take about eight hours for me to go through the proceedings, but I want you to give a second thought to it before I squeeze out the life of an innocent person, for this may have a negative repercussion on you as well,' cautioned the astrologer, who maintained his poise and demeanour.

'That, you leave it to me. I can take care of myself,' asserted Arjun,.

'It'll cost you a minimum of three lakhs,' said the astrologer, looking at him sceptically.

'I can give you half the amount now and the rest by a post-dated cheque,' said Arjun and went to his car to bring the packet containing the crisp notes.

The astrologer accepted it with a smug smile and Arjun left, elated, with a deep, relieved sigh.

CHAPTER TWENTY-NINE

After Babu left, Neema's emotions that had gathered like stormy clouds within exploded at last in loud, uncontrollable sobs until her heaving chest felt lighter for having unburdened all the pent-up sorrow of a lifetime. The truth had come into the open. It having been validated by a legitimate source verbally purged her from the gloom that had wrapped her in bitter loneliness and scepticism.

She finally declared, looking at her friend with her puffed-up eyes, 'I'm going to walk out now and live life according to my own terms.'

Sneha who was standing, stooped and put her arms around her friend, 'Look at me, darling. I'm happy being independent. I own a nursery. I make good business out of my beautiful plants. There is nothing to be afraid of, if you decide so.'

Neema looked up into her eyes with a broad smile curling her lips and asked in a low, husky voice, 'Won't I have trouble from other bad men?'

'Oh! My God, Time to shuck out the fear you are plagued with. One man who you trusted has done you more harm than all the other men you do not trust.'

'Life is an awful, ugly place not to have a best friend,' Neema remarked. Sneha looked down into Neema's eyes with a broad smile, having understood what she meant.

'Life has mocked us, but we together are going to mock at its silly cruelty,' said Sneha in an impelling tone. Pushing away the thought that marched inside her head, she snapped her fingers hurriedly and said, 'Let's get dressed. Goldie will be early today. We'll go out and party,'

Her doubt, whether Neema had the mood to go out and enjoy or not, was soon washed away when Neema got up, threw her arms around Sneha, and agreed to go out.

They drove fifteen kilometres at dusk, stylishly dressed, and Goldie sat in the backseat, overcome with excitement. She was telephoning her friends to tell them that she was on her way to a five-star luxury hotel for dinner with her mom and an aunty.

They chose a window table overlooking the pool. Huge crystal chandeliers hung from the high ceiling. There were little groups of foreigners on other far-off tables. Goldie was all smiles, thoroughly enjoying the soft Western music that was playing in the background. A heart-shaped menu card was given to each of them by a fair, cute-faced guy with a pleasant smile who looked especially at Goldie.

'Mom, please,' she whispered. 'I'll have a cocktail. They add very little gin, you know. I'm in college. I'm a big girl now.' She sounded very decisive.

Neema stared at Goldie with a glum face while the thought that ran in her mind was, *did I get anything in my life for having spurned all the joys of life? Stifling my passion and desires has only snuffed out my spirits.*

'I think we have to return the bar menu card,' she said aloud on purpose. Goldie glared at her. Neema looked at Sneha and said, 'I'll have white wine and Goldie . . .'

Abruptly, the young girl gave a name, looking at the card, and Sneha ordered the drinks joyfully, followed by a sumptuous dinner.

When they strolledthrough the breezy, cheerful garden leisurely, it was half past ten. Neema, who always took the precaution of getting back to home before ten at nightsurprisingly felt safe. Tonight, it was different. She let her hair down and was determined to free herself from a drab, meaningless marital life. Moreover, Sneha, who was bolder, was with her.

A lone woman with a long, sharp nose and a sharp chin was sipping beer on a garden chair at the far end, near a rose bush. Thoughts of a lone woman's struggles and miseries drifted through Sneha's mindas her eyes casually wandered in the lone woman's direction. She suddenly stopped Neema and whispered, 'Doesn't she look like Aparna?'

Neema, spellbound, let her eyes wander in the direction of the woman again. 'That's how she looks,' she said with a vague smile, unable to confirm.

Thin and tall, she was sitting cross-legged far away from the fountain pool in a darker corner, where the short decorative lamppost cast only a sidled pale white pool of light, casting her long shadow on the lawn. She was dressed in a one-shoulder, sexy aqua blue, body-hugging short dress. Neema and Sneha exchanged doubtful, surprised looks. *Was that Aparna, their old campus darling friend drinking and dining alone?* Stopping by the beautiful chrysanths, Neema gaped with wide, excited eyes.

'We need to find out,' Sneha said and they started walking towards her. The lady was staring into nothingness and seemed to be engrossed in her own world.

No sooner had they approached her table than the lady threw a nervous glance at them and a quizzical half smile. Sneha looked at her directly and asked openly, with a doubtful smile, 'Aren't you Aparna?'

The latter's face slowly blossomed. Recognition of her long lost friends began to show in her eyes. A bounteous smile lit up her face within seconds and her hand went up to cover her lips, which parted with unbelievable excitement. Tears of happiness ran down their cheeks as they got locked in each other's arms, each instantly convinced that fate had blessed them. Goldie, who was hovering behind them, beaming with a smile, was assured that she now had another loving aunty.

They sat in a circle, chatted and giggled, and ordered fresh fruit drinks. Aparna suddenly looked very cheerful. She laughed a great deal and said that it was a lucky evening for her, which she hadn't expected in the least. Her light-headedness, her merry talk, and her gait when she got up made it obvious that Aparna was inebriated. One oral invitation to go home with them was enough to toss her into their friendly circle. They screamed into the cool air with delight and happiness as they drove home at midnight.

The girls squeezed into the queen-sized bed and fell asleep.

After Goldie left the next morning, they sat at the dining table with coffee and breakfast and told Aparna everything about themselves.

When it was Aparna's turn, she began to laugh wildly. It soon gave way to tears. She had eloped because her brother had refused to accept her boyfriend as part of their family.

'Reality is so different from a phantasmal world, you know,' she said. 'We went to his native town in Orissa. Rented a small place with great difficulty. I took up a job as a schoolteacher.' She paused and smirked. 'For a pittance. A year passed, but he was jobless and he wasn't serious about it. I give birth to a baby boy. There have been nights when we had to sleep hungry.' Tears flowed down her face as she cast a look at Neema and Sneha, who were intently listening with glum faces. Rubbing her trickling nose with the back of her palm, Aparna started to laugh again. 'I left him and came back to my brother. Begged for forgiveness. Fortunately, he took me in. I took the bank exam and became a finance officer, but was foolish enough to take another man into my life who was my own caste and spoke my own Kannada language. I need to have someone in my life, you know. I can't stay with my brother's family my whole life.'

'Where is your son?' they asked in unison with an expression of concern.

Aparna got up, sighed, sipped a mouthful of water, and leaned forward on the dining table with her palms over its edge. 'He is in Orissa with my ex-husband.' Tears started pouring down from her eyes. 'My in-laws wouldn't give me the child. He should be around twenty now. Two years back, I went to Orissa looking for him, but the house itself didn't exist.'

Tears quivered in Sneha and Neema's eyes.

In an effort to divert Aparna's attention, they hastily asked, 'What happened to this Kannada guy?'

'On the day of our marriage, this guy tells me that he is impotent. That . . . that he is suffering from ED, erectile dysfunction. When he admitted the truth, I didn't want to go ahead and get married to him.' Aparna shrugged her shoulders, slumped on the chair, and closed her eyes, her mouth quivering.

While Sneha gathered Aparna in her arms and sat hugging her on the couch in the living room, Neema came with a tray full of fruits and coffee.

'The story doesn't end there,' Aparna said and looked at her friends.

Her soft, black eyes had dulled to such an extent that Neema suggested that she go to bed that instant, but Aparna spoke on. 'I shut my ass and agreed to marry a guy of my brother's choice for the third time. Just three months after marriage, he started forcing me to sleep with his friends for extra money, because he was greedy for money. He complained that his private business as a chartered accountant was not enough to realise his dream of building a mansion. I walked out of his house after a month's suffering, lodged a police complaint, and have now filed for a divorce.'

'So, you live with your brother now?' asked Sneha.

'Nope.' Aparna cast a downward look and said in a plain tone, 'He died in an accident while he was riding a scooter about four months ago.'

'Where do you live now?' they asked.

'I've rented a studio apartment, but I'm so afraid of living alone. Not safe. Tell me,' she said slowly in a woeful tone, 'am I to be blamed for all that happened in my life?'

'Nope, who says so?' said Sneha in a fiery tone. 'You wanted to settle down as a housewife, but fate was not kind to you.'

'That's not your fault,' added Neema.

'My relatives, my colleagues, my neighbours. All feel that I'm the bad character,' said Aparna. 'According to them, I do not know how to manage situations. I do not conform to the standards laid down in our Indian scriptures of being the submissive, good wife. I do not know the art of getting along with a husband.' She paused reflectively and continued, 'People do not invite me for functions. My neighbours do not invite me on pooja occasions, and my relatives do not see me anymore.'

Aparna was drained of all cheerfulness that had sprung on her face in the hotel.

'Honey,' Sneha said at length, 'the world you spoke of now has no time to do anything good. People are busy with their own lives. Now, why don't you get busy with your own? We have found each other at last. Neema, you, and I—don't we make a family?'

Aparna's face suddenly lit up with a newfound joy. The three stood up and locked themselves in each other's arms. They ordered food from a nearby restaurant and sat chatting about a number of things. When Sneha squatted on the floor and began to hiccup, they started to laugh hysterically with tears in their eyes, just like the old times. Over their dinner, it was decided that they buy or rent a house and live together.

Their fun and conversation was curiously watched and recorded by Arjun and Priya. Tara and Shravana also had gathered as usual in the dingy apartment.

It was decided that Arjun would go back home that evening.

'I want to show her friends that I'm the goody-goody husband,' he told Priya as he got ready to leave. He dropped Priya at home before he started driving towards his own.

Around quarter to eleven, Goldie, who was speaking with a friend in the cool night's breeze, saw from the balcony her dad's car pull up in front of the house. She flew down the stairs and broke the news with ruffled emotions to the trio, who were happily watching one of Bobby Deol's movies. Confounded glances skirted around. Switching off the television, the three women jumped up from the couch like three little girls, rushed into the bedroom, and locked themselves in; nervous as to the commotion the man might create with strangers in his house.

Goldie quickly picked up a book and sat studiously at the dining table. When she heard the key turn in the hole and the sound of his boot crossing the threshold, her face tightened, for here was a stranger she hardly related to as a father. He had not been home for almost a fortnight, nor had he made any effort to talk to her at least over the phone, even to enquire about her well-being.

He passed her by the side of the table and started to climb the stairs, noticing slyly that Neema's door was closed, and knew for sure that she was with her friends. Pausing abruptly at his door, he half-turned with a smile and said louder than his usual pitch, 'Hi, Goldie, how are you? You didn't even look at me.' She lifted up her face and, sensing sharply the falsity of his gesture with the ugly pout of his thick, wide, slimy lips, feigned a smile with a puckered mouth. 'I'm good. How are you, Dad?' she asked with equanimity.

'Where is your mom?' he asked, sounding very concerned.

'In her room,' Goldie answered with her face bent on her text.

Inside the room, the three women stood in different places with tightness in their throats. Aparna, clad in her shorts and a T-shirt, had shut her eyes tight and was counting every step as he climbed with his boots on. Neema, in her light pink chudidar, was standing on the other side of the bed with her hands on her wide-open mouth, trying to allay an obscure fear, and Sneha, in pyjamas and a crepe, floral top, appeared to be slightly shaken, with her hands on her chest.

Within moments, they began to giggle, involuntarily and soundlessly, looking at each other and being thus frightened for no apparent reason. Suddenly, they heard urgent knocks on the door. Aparna threw her eyes wide open and the other two composed their faces to get the door. The knocks were immediately followed by Arjun's voice, which sounded absolutely caring. 'Neema, if you want an extra bed sheet, you can take it from my room.'

The ladies looked into each other's eyes sceptically. Sneha, who was composed and bolder than her friends croaked, 'Sure.'

'He probably knows we are here,' hissed Aparna.

'Hmm,' agreed Neema. 'Why did he say extra bed sheet?'

'Something fishy,' whispered Sneha.

After some fifteen minutes, Goldie called her mom on her mobile from her room and said in an excited tone,

'He is in his room, Mom, today. By the way, I called to say goodnight to you all.'

'Go to sleep, baby. Goodnight from me and my friends,' said Neema reassuringly.

'Neema.' They heard his voice again at their bedroom door, suffused with love, when they had just switched off the light and gotten into bed. 'I've kept a jug of water on the dining table just in case you need it.' This time, Aparna, gathering up her courage, cooed 'Sure' and again, the three began to shake involuntarily with muted laughter.

In the morning, Goldie nimbly knocked on their bedroom and greeted them with coffee and a loud good morning. 'He is gone,' she announced with a big smile.

CHAPTER THIRTY

Babu, who had taken the afternoon bus after having met Neema reached Hassan on time and was home in the evening for the aromatic filtered coffee prepared by his mother. He narrated to her everything that he had gone through and explained why he had hurried home without making her a phone call.

Jayamma, who at first chided him for the risk he had taken unnecessarily and for interfering in the life of someone who belonged to the upper class of society, softened towards her son for the pity and sympathy he had shown for a young woman who was being cheated on.

He got back to his work as usual the next day and met all his friends and told them unbelievable stories about the metropolitan city, but discreetly held back from disclosing anything about Arjun or his family. To defame Arjun would have a malefic effect on Neema, too, and he had no intention of slandering the name of a family who he had known for years as good neighbours. Defaming a reputed, honourable family who had once been tolerably good to his mother was the last thing he could think of.

'Where had you been?' they asked him curiously, and Babu had a lot to tell in general about the big city and the lifestyle of the rich folks and the undisclosed woes of even educated women who lived in big houses. Not once did he mention Arjun's name.

The day was bright and beautiful. He didn't go back to work after lunch for he wanted to take his mother out for a matinee. He had missed his mother for so long and he wanted to spend time with her.

In the evening, around quarter to seven, he took his auto and went on his usual routine, telling his mother that he would return soon. When he was just counting on returning home for dinner, he started to feel breathless. His auto parked in front of a temple, he sat pale and unable to drive.

Another driver who had pulled his auto close to Babu's was appalled to see his friend being breathless.

'What happened, Babu?' He hopped out of his auto but his words sounded remote to Babu, as if they were coming from a far-off distance. Babu's eyeballs had almost disappeared behind his upper lids as he sat with his head tilted back and gasped for breath. Very soon, autos stopped by and a group of drivers milled around Babu's vehicle. They put him in the backseat and cradled his head. Someone lifted a bottle of water to his mouth, but he looked alarmingly weak and famished and unable to gulp down the liquid. He was now struggling to breathe, pulling air in short breaths with grunts. Animated discussions went around, and without wasting further time, two drivers quickly jumped to the front seat and started to drive wildly. Two more in the backseat were holding Babu in their arms. No sooner had they reached Babu's house than they screamed for Jayamma to hurry out. She ran in and brought a glass of water, but her son's hands hung limp on either side and his eyes were half-closed. He was drawing air in short gasps.

One of the drivers suggested they rush him to the local pundit, who was not only well-versed in herbal medicines but was a clairvoyant and a black magician, as well. Jayamma sat in the backseat; her son gathered in her arms with tears streaming down her face, while two drivers sharing the front seat sped hysterically past the few quiet streets and swung the auto close to the pundit's house. They lifted Babu, carried him inside the small house in panic, and no time was wasted, either, by the middle-aged kind pundit who quickly scrutinised Babu, and concluded that it was the result of black magic.

Babu was immediately shifted to a semi-dark private chamber and the pundit closed the door, banning the entry of others. They, however, waited outside restlessly, discussing how it had all happened. Since Babu had explained everything to his mother, it slowly dawned on Jayamma who this miscreant could be. She sat on a bench outside weeping uncontrollably while two of Babu's close friends stood on either side of her, comforting her. After a wait of two tension-filled hours, the pundit emerged outside and broke the news that Babu was out of danger.

It was past midnight when they brought Babu safely back home.

CHAPTER THIRTY-ONE

Sneha, Neema, and Aparna had happily neglected their official work for almost a week. Their unconditional support, non-judgemental attitude, and the unrestrained love they had adopted for each other as college girls on the campus stood them in good stead even in their adulthood, which helped them bounce back to bubbly life in each other's company, like old times. Their sense of loss and loneliness had disappeared like ash in the wind and their ennui had melted like ice. Invigorated and revitalised, on Monday morning, they donned their lipstick and got ready to get back to their work. They vowed to keep in touch and never to feel alone. It was the beginning of the week and the roads were unusually crowded. The usual road that Neema took had jam-packed traffic moving at a snail's speed, forcing her to take the anfractuous, uneven, un-macadamised bylanes to reach town hall, which was halfway down the main road to her college. Yet getting stuck in the mile-long traffic was inevitable.

After a restless twenty-minute wait, she telephoned Sneha, who instantly screamed with delight that Milan's photo was in the newspapers and that her repeated calls to

Neema had failed due to unknown reasons. Neema held the phone between her left ear and shoulder and with her right hand on the steering wheel gave an astonished smile and was hardly able to say anything, gripped by unbelievable surprise and nervous excitement.

She finally asked sceptically in a tiny tone, 'Why is Milan in the papers?' as she let her car jerk forward inch by inch.

'Tomorrow evening, he is delivering a speech on new trends in global education in, in, in a five-star hotel,' Sneha stammered with choked excitement. Neema cut the phone, for traffic had picked up to the normal speed. A row of ministers' cars zoomed past her with irrational speed.

Her mind unconsciously rambled to the past. Milan had expressed his love for her openly when he had met her years ago in her college. But she had been too busy with the turmoil of her own life to telephone him even on his birthday. *Would he forgive me at all if I met him now?* She recalled his handsome face and winsome smile with a deep fondness, one who had always been the protagonist of her romantic dreams. A thin film of tears rose in her eyes and clouded her vision as she accelerated in the moving traffic.

It was Aparna next who was screaming over the phone when Neema was turning off the key in the parking lot. She said that she had telephoned because she had something special to tell Neema. She was all glee when she broke the news that Milan's speech was in Hotel International at 6 p.m. the next evening and that she had already requested a press reporter to reserve seats for the three of them. 'We are not going to miss this opportunity. It is our old friend, Milan, you see.'

Neema was tongue-tied. She giggled and disconnected the phone. Aparna knew that Neema wouldn't have found her voice to speak.

Neema was delighted to hear the news from her friends. *Of course! I can't miss the opportunity of seeing Milan after so many years. Would he be with his wife and children? Was he happy in his marriage? When and who would he have married?* Questions she couldn't wait to get answers clouded her mind as she walked to her staff room. The next three hours she spent in the college was in nervous anticipation of her possible meeting with Milan the next day.

Arjun also was stuck in the traffic. He was on his way to the hospital to meet Kanthi. He had asked Priya to redact the one important document that mentioned a transfer of fifty lakhs from Kanthi's financial resources to his account more so as a gift, he being her favourite son-in-law, rather than for his legal services Moving at snail's speed, he checked whether all the papers were intact. The other document said that Kanthi was now the sole heir to all movable and immovable properties left behind by her father-in-law. He had carefully introduced the words 'deceased' and 'childless' as descriptive words with reference to the brother-in-law, who lived in the village. He had also made another document, a will on behalf of Kanthi that said that all her property would go to Mili after her death, except for the purple-coloured embroidered chudidar that solely belonged to Neema.

Little tremors of laughter rumbled in his stomach as he thought of Babu's graveyard, the money he would be getting and freedom from Neema's bondage forever. All that Arjun needed was Kanthi's signature on the papers. He walked down the spacious but chilly, spic-and-span corridor of the hospital with a battery of thoughts barraging him.

A nurse greeted him and led him into Kanthi's room. A dim smile hovered on Kanthi's lips when she saw her son-in-law. There were no signs of her fully recuperating. She lay there, weak and pale with her eyes open. The intravenous fluid did its silent job. She could move her limbs slowly, and he knew she could sign.

Sitting on the edge of her bed, he showed her the papers eagerly and explained to her the draft and certain risks involved in it. Without any protest, she signed with fiercely shaking hands even those papers that made him instantly rich by fifty lakhs. Leaving all the other papers on the bedside metal table, Arjun got up with his own precious document, picked up an orange too, and left exultantly with a huge smile that he couldn't suppress till he reached his office.

But his joy seemed to be short-lived. No sooner had he reached his office in Gandhi bazaar than the telephone on his table started to ring.

'My son is alive, you bastard,' Jayamma screamed with fury from the other end. 'Your dad had used the same trick to kill one of his clients, you shameless dog.' She hung up the phone. She had not given him time to answer or protest. She had called from a booth, and Arjun didn't have her number to call back. His face went white in utter shock and dismay. He sat there with trembling hands before he tried Babu's number, but it was switched off.

Jayamma had rushed to Bangalore after her son had recouped from shock and weakness. That morning, along with her son, she had left Hassan determined to lodge a complaint with the police. But her first priority was to meet ailing Kanthi.

They telephoned Neema's house and learnt from Goldie that Kanthi was still in the hospital, recovering very slowly and within an hour, they were in the hospital.

Jayamma introduced herself to the doctor, saying that she was Kanthi's elder sister. Kanthi had been given an injection and was in a deep state of sleep. Jayamma stood by her bed and wondered whether she knew anything at all about the shady life of Arjun.

Babu, who hovered close by, gradually got curious about the white sheets of papers that were fluttering on the side table. They were folded in half lengthwise, and he couldn't resist glancing at them again and again until his eyes caught Kanthi's signature from within the folds.

He took the papers and slipped out. He walked to the adjacent building and sat down, curiously going through them. He closed his eyes and rested his pounding head on the back of the seat. So Kanthi was the abettor. He made photocopies of all the sheets and went back to Kanthi's room. She was not yet awake. He took his mother's arm and dragged her outside.

Jayamma refused to go. She wanted an explanation from her son. Babu said he would explain and took his mother to the hospital canteen, showed her the papers, and made her understand everything as they ate. It was unbelievable. Jayamma couldn't believe her ears that Kanthi could get involved in such a heinous crime. She insisted that it was absolutely necessary to talk to her.

When they returned, the nurse said that Kanthi had been shifted to the ICU again, as she had suddenly developed a breathing problem. It was only Jayamma who was permitted to go inside. Babu went to the other room and put the papers back on the same table.

Jayamma stood by her friend's bed and asked her point-blank, 'Why did you wrong your own daughter, Kanthi?' *This woman whom she had known from her childhood had not been kind to her own daughter?* That was incredible and shocking to Jayamma. She thought it right to get an explanation before Kanthi died, although her moral beliefs were against it.

Kanthi looked at her from the top of her breathing pipe. She plucked it and said slowly, breathing hard, her eyes fixed on the ceiling, 'I know I have been wrong. But I hated her from the beginning.'

Jayamma searched in her eyes for an explanation. Kanthi had slipped back the breathing equipment on her nose again. It almost covered her mouth. There was nothing for Jayamma to say, nothing to feel. It was implausible that Kanthi, whom she had known as a simple Mysore girl, could foster such bitter hatred for her own daughter. 'Why did you hate your own daughter, Kanthi?' she couldn't resist asking.

'She took away half of my husband's love and I could never forgive her for that,' Kanthi mumbled with difficulty. She removed and slid the air mask back to her nostrils, unable to speak further through her short spasms of breath.

There were so many things Jayamma wanted to say. So many things to expound, so many things to construe for the edification of the poorly indoctrinated woman, one who was like her own sister. But all that was useless for one who was dying. Things could not be reverted. What had happened could not be undone. She put her hand on Kanthi's arm in sympathy and turned back. But she was weeping fiercely. When she came out of the ICU, the nurse told her that Mili had not turned up for the past couple of days and insisted that someone stay with the patient. Jayamma was weeping bitterly. She said she would make some arrangement and left with Babu. There were so many reasons for her tears, all of which she couldn't explain to her son.

After she emerged out of the hospital feeling low and shaken, with Babu following her, she telephoned Neema to tell her everything. Neema begged her to visit in person, to which she conceded.

Jayamma and Babu came to Neema's house that evening.

'You cannot expect to repair your marriage, honey,' Jayamma told her over dinner. She and Babu told her everything that had happened and also revealed to her about the property that her mother had inherited and the will that was made by Arjun himself in favour of Mili.

'Your husband is dangerous. It would be better for you to separate. You will always have my son's and my support,' Jayamma said tenderly.

Goldie sat on the couch and listened to everything that Jayamma and Babu were saying and wondered what strength her mother might possess to have undergone all this bitterness in life.

To marry or not to marry loomed large in her mind.

CHAPTER THIRTY-TWO

After Jayamma's call, Arjun hadn't been able to concentrate on his job. He didn't attend to any court matter, but sat thinking of options to extricate himself from the complicate situation that had risen. In the evening, he, Shravana, and their bimbos huddled together on the bed under the roaring fan sipping chilled beer in their dingy room and watched Jayamma and Babu taking leave of Neema. Finally, things had come to a boil. Arjun's evilness had come to light.

Around nine o'clock, the next morning, the four decided to head to Azad Nagar, a remote suburb of Bangalore that was predominated by the bourgeois class. Locating the house they were looking for was not easy. Many years ago, somebody had given the address to Shravana and he had ferreted it out now from one of his old diaries.

After encountering some difficulty in the morning rush hour traffic, they finally succeeded in spotting it based on the description that Bheema, the person they were soon going to encounter, had given them over the phone.

One house in the compact row of almost look-alike houses had a freshly painted green compound wall. It was a double-storied building with a bigger front yard with cement flooring and a row of healthy rose bushes along the length of its compound wall. The black dual driveway gates were closed and on first sight, it looked as if there were no occupants in the building.

They pushed open the metal gate and nervously climbed the external concrete stairs adjoining the house. The house downstairs was closed, but voices of women and children could be heard through the open window as they climbed.

Upstairs, the door to their right was widely open and two well-built, middle-aged men, one with a thick moustache and the other with a goatee beard and a skull cap, were seated at a writing table opposite each other in conversation. They looked relaxed, their white mull kurtas and checkered lungis fluttering in the cool breeze that blew from outside in spite of the rising heat of the day. As soon as they saw the two men and the two ladies under their little porch, they got up readily with a smile ushered them in and led them into a wider hall inside.

As soon as they were seated on the settee, Bheema, the guy with the black moustache, looked at Arjun and asked politely albeit his terrific built, 'What will you have, sir?'

Arjun turned to his friend Shravana for an answer, and the latter tittered before he said, 'You decide, boy.' The very fact that he was in an underworld don's house had rendered Shravana in astriction.

'Beer will do,' replied Arjun and added, gesturing towards the ladies, 'Some soft drink for them.'

Another plain-looking younger man in a pair of ankle length white pyjamas and a white kurta, who was hovering behind the doors, came out with a tray of glasses and bottles. Almost at the same time, the boss, Azad, who had earned the name as the leader of the area for nefarious activities, emerged from a closet that was at the farthest set-back niche behind Bheema.

Arjun and Shravana shifted their bodies slightly in their chairs. As he strode towards them, he hemmed deeply and loudly, eyeing his white full arm sleeve that he was rolling up. Adjusting his white skull cap, he sat on the leather couch beside Bheema. He was six feet tall, well-built, and looked very strong. Pyrex water glasses were soon filled with drinks. The man with the goatee and the plain-looking assistant who actually wielded the guns and knives disappeared from the scene.

'An AK-124 will do,' said Bheema, turning to Azad. Azad nodded, looking only at the glasses with an understanding sly smile. A black mole on his brunette face just above his left eyebrow, his red, drunken eyes, the sarcastic smile that hovered on his mouth, his gross, auburn goatee and a coarse moustache and the way he sat with his legs sprawled, spoke every inch of the cool manner in which he executed his villainous activities.

Though he had been in jail twice, serving almost a year each time he was arrested, nothing had stopped him from continuing with his underworld activities, for it was said that he was protected by some politicians among whom he had become popular. He was caught twice—once for having murdered a jeweller in broad daylight, hacking him to death under the railway bridge, and the second time for slashing the throat of a businessman in his office.

'Hope Bheema has told you. Twenty lakhs now and twenty after the job is done,' he said in a calm and collected manner to Arjun in his deep, baritone voice. Arjun readily drew a packet from his trouser pocket and thrust it at him.

'Shukriya,' Azad grunted and passed it to the man with the goatee who had now come out and was standing beside him. He accepted the packet and disappeared once again.

'She leaves home around eight thirty in the morning and takes the flyover to reach her college,' said Arjun.

'A drive of about twelve kilometres from the house to her college,' added Shravana with a nervous laugh.

'Don't worry, sir. We are used to daylight hacking,' assured Bheema.

The bimbos were sipping their drinks and watching in awe. Finally, the four got up and left with exalted feelings.

They couldn't wait for the next day to broach.

CHAPTER THIRTY-THREE

Bheema and his plain-looking aide Irfan left rather early in the morning.

Lying in wait in their luxurious AC Ford, they spotted Neema's car emerging from the by lane and take the main flyover. They pulled the gear and in a jiffy were after her. They watched her car merge with the traffic near the town hall. Some two-wheeler guys overtook the Ford and wedged between her car and theirs, to their greatest annoyance.

'Look out, look out. Don't lose sight of her car,' barked Bheema, handling the steering wheel.

They raced behind her car, which was winding its way among the rush hour traffic. Irfan stuck out his hand, motioning for someone behind to slow down, while Bheema honked and yelled through the window at those who were trying to overtake them. In a minute, they lost her car. Though they sped with difficulty, putting their lives at risk, they were unable to catch up in the heavy traffic for which Bangalore is notorious for.

Irfan, who was frantically searching for her car through the windows, suddenly sighted it entering her college campus and being parked in a slot among others. They were still on the other side of the traffic lane when she entered her college.

No outside vehicles were allowed inside the college premises. Furious and annoyed, they drove into the spacious parking lot of the imperial stone building, a government officers' enclave on the opposite side, and waited.

After three hours, Irfan got out and came back with some buns, fruits, and tea, and settled down again in his seat. Though they felt drowsy in the sunny afternoon, they got themselves some more tea and kept vigil.

Around four o'clock in the afternoon, Neema ducked into her car, and drove towards the other gate, a furlong away from the main building of her college. She safely merged with the traffic and headed to Sneha's nursery, which was close to Cubbon Park.

At five past four, Bheema craned his neck and struggled to get a view of the parking lot inside the college campus. Ironically, many slots had cleared up.

'You dozing dog!' Bheema barked, turning towards his aide and slapping Irfan on the cheek wokehim up. The young man hopped out anxiously and crossed the perpetually traffic-ridden road overwrought with rabid angst and enquired with the security at the college gate about Neema's Maruthi. The security checked the slot and replied that the car had left. They did not waste another second. Piqued at their inattentiveness and fuming at Irfan for neglecting his duty, Bheema sped at a speed of forty kilometres in the growing evening traffic and was just in time to catch a glimpse of the red vehicle that was heading towards a by lane next to Cubbon Park. They caught her disappearing into a huge, posh building when they lurched in front of the adjacent coffee shop. It was not before a full forty minutes that they saw Neema emerge with fresh make-up, laughing cheerfully in a gorgeous chiffon sari, her hair let down in soft curls. She was carrying a rose plant. They didn't know who the other lady, dressed almost similarly, was.

The ladies walked to the car and drove off. Irfan and Bheema were once again hot on the automobile's wheels. Neema's car stopped near an icecream parlour on Grand Road, and a third lady, dressed chicly in a nylon sari and wearing a large smile, came out of a bank and got into the car. Bheema followed them at full speed as the red hatchback sped straight ahead towards Hotel International.

The ladies were met at the gate by a smart young man, the reporter of an important television news channel. They switched off the AC and cranked down their windows just a little for breeze. Bheema smacked Irfan's hand who had readied himself with the gun.

'Look at the politicians there. You mad dog,' Bheema barked, 'an important function or something like that.' He drove into the parking lot and said, 'I'll wait here. You go and before the function starts, just use the silencer and shoot her in the crowd and flee from the place.' Irfan twirled his moustache with his thumb and forefinger, got out of the car, tweaked his white cotton kurta, and was close on the trio's heels.

The reporter escorted the ladies to the beautifully decorated, brightly lit huge conference hall and handed each of them a glossy leaflet that informed them about the programme that was to begin shortly.

. Milan's handsome face smiled back at them from the leaflet. He was there to deliver a lecture as an educational consultant. The hall was already packed with people, young and old, delighted to be attending a talk by one who had travelled to many countries and ran a successful business of his own in the United States.

There were jubilant claps when Milan appeared on the stage. There was an air of dignity and professionalism when he stood there holding the microphone, dressed smartly in a Brooks Brothers suit. The ladies sat dumbstruck with half-choked throats. They were listening to their classmate, Milan, who was a shy guy on the campus years ago. He looked even more handsome with the little weight he had put on.

He was talking something about sectarianism and world peace. He was narrating some interesting anecdotes from the time when he had worked with the International Red Cross. As he scanned the rows of people, all curious and attentive, his eyes fell on Neema and the two other long-lost friends who had faded out of his life. With a momentary quivering stir of emotion that darted through his heart, he shifted his legs, hemmed, cast a darting look towards the floor of the dais, rubbed the tip of his nose once, and continued with a smile, his gaze, unobtrusively, wandering between Neema and the other girls.

'We hold regular programmes on discipline, behaviour, and classroom management issues. We are interested in students' welfare. Exchange programmes are vital not only to students, but also . . .'

Suddenly, a few people sprang up and began to scream. As Milan gasped and hopped from the podium, he caught a man running to the exit. Sneha and Aparna started screaming frantically as they knelt beside Neema, who had collapsed from the gunshot. Milan calmed them down and made urgent calls for the ambulance. The protection officer rushed out with his radio. A troop of other officers and local policemen darted behind him, but they couldn't spot anybody carrying or holding a gun or even moving with suspicious behaviour.

Irfan and Bheema sat in their car in the parking lot with their heads bent down over a newspaper. Guards rushed about with bandages, cotton rolls and water while terrified people gathered around Neema, who had swooned. She had a bullet in her shoulder and was bleeding profusely. Milan knelt, cradling Neema's head on his lap. Sneha and Aparna, who knelt on either side of Neema, were all tears and were torn emotionally. Within minutes, a doctor and nurses arrived and Milan offered to go with them in the ambulance and told his protection officer that he would be fine.

Albeit the comforting words he was offering to Sneha and Aparna, he realised the hollowness that he was experiencing inside at seeing Neema unconscious. He had always loved her and he loved her still. His beloved

Neemawho he felt had always been enigmatic. He rubbed her brow now and sat with the back of his hand on her cheek. He knew that her friends were aware of theinconspicuous bond that had developed between him and Neema on the campus long ago.

Milan scuttled between his official duties and the luxurious hospital from the base of his five-star hotel for three days until Neema had fully recouped and was ready to be discharged. The girls told him about their lives and he in turn revealed that he had never gotten married. Marriage didn't interest him, he said. However, he told them that he was still interested in making Neema a happy person. She lay in her bed in her own bedroom, listening to them, low and weak and happy to have them all there. Goldie stayed by her mama's side and took care of her medication.

Nevertheless, to her joy, Sneha and Aparna coaxed Goldie not to miss her classes and pampered her with a love that no less equalled that of Neema's.

CHAPTER THIRTY-FOUR

Irfan and Bheema had failed utterly for the first time. They begged Arjun to give them one more chance. Meanwhile, Arjun threatened Azad to give him back his money.

Arjun and Priya fled Bangalore and checked into a resort on the outskirts of the city. Shravana informed him over the phone that no 'Khakis,' referring to the police, had raised an alarm yet.

Late evening, Arjun raised a toast, stripped his clothes, and started to kiss Priya. He sensed something unusual in the movement of his mouth. As the goblet dropped from his hand, strewing the carpet with its fragments, he collapsed onto the bed with his face down, his legs sticking out. He tried to lift himself up, but his head began to jerk to the right involuntarily. His mouth twisted and his green eyeballs rolled in the pools of his white retina like a man possessed of some demon.

Priya shrieked in aberration and watched aghast as his limbs twisted and went out of shape. 'Arjun! What happened?' Priya squealed. Her eyes were wide with fear and bewilderment as she hunkered down and caught him by the shoulder. He vainly tried to fix his eyes on her, but her cries vaguely reached his ears, as if from a far-off distance. She rushed to the landline and called the doctor on service and immediately grabbed her mobile and frantically made a call for an ambulance. He lay on the bed, comatose.

When he was taken to the hospital, the doctor said that he had had a stroke and needed to be kept in the Intensive Care Unit.

#

Neema tried to get back on her legs on the fourth day after her discharge. She tried Arjun's number, but it was unreachable.

Her friends wanted to celebrate her recovery, although Neema was anxious to go and visit her mother. They promised to accompany her to the hospital after the party was over. Milan's protection officer stood guard in front of their house, and Goldie was flattered.

That evening, rap songs were played and a huge cake was ordered. The benefit of cutting the cake was given to Goldie, who enjoyed all the pampering and attention she received. While they were animatedly talking about their lives, Aparna was engrossed in a magazine and kept flicking its pages curiously.

'Who has caught your attention?' asked Neema, as she had taken notice of her friend's disassociation from the group's lively chat.

Goldie grabbed the magazine as Aparna was grinning at her and, standing in the centre of the living room, read loudly from its pages: From Jamaica. A reggae dancehall artist. Sean Paul, recipient of achievement award in 1964. She turned the magazine towards them and showed them all the picture of Sean Paul.

Neema and Sneha stared at the handsome guy on the page and began to laugh.

'You want to go to Jamaica?' they teased Aparna. She sat in a huff and went upstairs, blushing, with Goldie. Sneha too excused herself and scuttled up the stairs.

Just as they had guessed, Milan moved close to the sofa on which Neema was sitting. She stood up instantly, her dignity and her bashfulness being her permanent apparel. Milan held her by the wrist and looked deep into her eyes with emotion.

'Will you marry me, Neema?' he asked her earnestly, going down on his knees and impersonating a suitor with a rose in his hand.

A smile broke on Neema's face and she met his loving eyes. She put her arms around his neck in her moment of emotion, coaxed him to rise, and instantly surrendered to his warm embrace, leaning her head on his chest.

He knew she was stubborn. And just as he had anticipated, she whispered, 'Milan, I adore you, but,' she looked up into his romantic eyes, 'my daughter needs me now more than ever and I may soon have a son-in-law walking about in my house.'

'Is Goldie not my daughter too?' he protested.

'At her age, she may not feel comfortable, Milan,' Neema said.

He looked at her little smile in silence. 'I'm trying to import the logical sense of yourwell-meant words,' he said at length, before he bent his head and pressed his lips to hers.

She received it for the first time, a kiss she had dreamed and imagined and yearned for in her life. Without a protest, she reciprocated.

'So soon, we are in our fifties. Time has flown by so quickly!' she sighed, resting her head on his chest.

'Youare my darling even in your fifties. You will be my darling forever,' he whispered, looking down romantically into her sensual eyes. 'One day, your daughter and son-in-law will be mine too,' he whispered.

She doubted if this most ecstatic moment would ever happen again in her life. She had rejected his proposal. Her craving to have a spouse in her life had strangely died down. However, the essence of her pleasure was in the very special feeling of belongingness, a feeling that was soporific to Neema. The fact that Milan would always be there for her was something in which she drifted with her eyes closed and her head pressed against his warm chest.

When the girls walked down, they split and Milan said cheerfully that he would soon be arranging for their visas so that they could visit him in America.

There were screams of joy and happiness in the air. There was more music and laughter and the cake and wine did its round again.

CHAPTER THIRTY-FIVE

Just then, Neema's mobile began to ring from an unknown number. She picked up the phone and glanced at her friends with quizzical eyebrows.

Milan grabbed the phone and switched on the speaker, suspicious of the nature of the call, an unknown number late at night?

It was a call from the police headquarters. The underworld dons had been arrested. Two persons by name Jayamma and Babu had given a written complaint inculpating Arjun, they said. They wanted Neema the next day for further clarification. Shortly afterwards, the phone buzzed again, and this time, it was from the hospital to let Neema know that her mother's condition was critical and that there was no family member with her.

Milan and the girls started off immediately. It was half past eleven and the officer who had stood guard drove the lancer.

Kanthi was lying, pathetically weak and pale, motionless, on oxygen support. She no more belonged to the world.

Her blank eyes moved in a disassociated manner towards Neema.

Tears welled in Neema's eyes. The doctors pronounced that Kanthi's end had come. Neema begged the doctor in charge to permit her to spoon-feed her mom with some water.

She held her mama's head in her lap and gave her a sip of the mineral water she had brought with her. Neema and her little gang stayed by Kanthi's bedside the whole night. Even before dawn could break, Kanthi was pronounced dead.

The doctor had finally been able to get Mili on the phone. Mili had just returned from a family holiday tour. She and her husband rushed to the hospital, though an hour late.

Milan, meanwhile, took charge of all the formalities that had to be done in the hospital. An autopsy was conducted before the cadaver was taken off to the electric crematorium.

There was no news about Arjun. Shravana and Tara, who had rushed to the multi-speciality hospital, a new branch in Hosur on the border of Bangalore, had switched off Arjun's mobile. A battery of tests was conducted on him, and he was lying unconscious. The police met Neema and her friends at the hospital itself, on Milan's suggestion. Neema told the police that she didn't have any clue as to the whereabouts of her husband, Arjun, nor did she know anything about the activities he was involved in.

Later that evening, they received news that Arjun had been found in the hospital in an unpredictable coma. However, he and his aides had been slammed with six years of imprisonment. While Azad, Bheema, and Irfan boldly showed their faces in the media, Shravana and his girls hid theirs behind their palms while they were whisked away by the police.

Neema telephoned Jayamma and broke all the sad tidings.

Milan left for America late that night. His little campus family saw him off at the airport, each giving him a warm hug.

CHAPTER THIRTY-SIX

The summer sun had vanished. Low, dark clouds hung above. Neema stood in the balcony and opened her arms like a child to feel the forceful blow of the gusty wind that had suddenly picked up. It was cool. She had faced all the other blows of life. With her eyes closed blissfully, she let the cold wind of the dark clouds osculate her ravenously. Swept onto her face with the sudden gale were the rushing, splashing drops of the rain that steadily picked up. Neema stepped back and stood under the porch.

The rain fell with a slanting gossamer touch. The dusty, heated air and the smell of the hot earth rose up with the first sheet of rain. The humid, muddy smell that wafted to her nose stirred her sensation in one glorious moment. It brought her an inexplicable sense of contentment. She was on her own like the happy little bird that fluttered in her garden in the mornings . Liberated and flying in her romantic chimera all by herself, shielded by the heavenly shower and wrapped in the warmth of her elated happiness.

Goldie brought a tray of coffee and stood beside her. She asked in a low tone if Neema would initiate any legal proceedings against her dad and his aides. Neema put her arm around the girl's shoulders and said complacently, 'As a man sows, so shall he reap.'

Goldie turned her head and stared into her mother's eyes with a taunting smile. 'You are a traditional mom from some Bible story.'

'Perhaps I am.' Neema smiled joyfully and rubbed the tip of her nose to Goldie's. 'My life is even shorter now. I have no time for revenge and hatred, baby.' She screwed up her nose and smiled.

Goldie scrunched her face, put her arm around her mama's waist, and started tickling her. 'You are a sweet mama,' she said at length. Neema threw away the sim card of her mobile and inserted the new one that Goldie had bought for her.

That night, Neema had the most enchanting dream she had ever seen –

Animals, both wild and the timid, drifted with wings from their abodes with serene faces, liberated from their confines, daring in their moves and yet harmless by nature; a spectacular riot of colours in the game park, all buoyant and sprightly. Little, colourful birds fluttered merrily far and near and perched on flowers and stems or rode on the gliding animals. Neema levitated like an angel with wings on her shoulders and sailed merrily in the gentle wind.

#

Four months later, Neema and her friends gathered in Taj West End to celebrate the receipt of their American visas.

They bought Goldie her favourite cocktail and ordered white wine for Neema, vodka for Aparna, and chilled beer for Sneha.

Neema gifted Aparna a bottle of Remy Martin VSOP, as the latter rambled excitedly about Sean Paul's Billboard Music Awards and his songs, sipping her champagne.

After they had finished their a la carte spread, Sneha pulled out a big packet from her handbag and presented Neema with a set of CDs of Bobby Deol's films and winked naughtily at her.

Neema screamed with joy. Soon, Aparna unfurled a roll of typed paper and held it up in front of Sneha. It was a contract that Sneha simply had to sign, agreeing to supply a dozen banks and educational institutions with flowers and plants from her nursery for an entire year. It was a contract she had always dreamt of. 'A gift of a lifetime!' she cried out in delight.

Shortly afterwards, they telephoned Milan and said that they would join him for Christmas. They heard his delighted voice exclaim that he couldn't wait to seethem.

The girls waited for December twentieth to embark on their exciting trip to the United States via Chennai. They hired a taxi on the D-day and drove to Marina beach to celebrate their happiness and independence.

Goldie stayed back, saying she couldn't miss a job interview that had come up.

EPILOGUE

A bright, full moon shone in the celestial sky that peaceful night. The three girls lay on the sands of the beach in the cool breeze, watching the glowing moon and enjoying their drinks with almost the same thought running in their minds that love and trust was all that mattered to make a family in contrast to the traditionally accepted forms of relationships.

The monstrous tides of the eternal sea rose and raged in its sheer, white glory and ebbed fiercely, lugging away the abandoned crushed tins and emptied covers. With it went the words of the girls, too, which they flung to the ocean spiritedly. 'We are not crapehangers anymore,' they screamed determinedly in unison and cried through laughter.

Standing tall and beautiful in a pair of blue jeans and fiercely fluttering white shirt, Sneha began yodelling Stephen C Foster's poem with a Coke in her hand:

Beautiful dreamer, wake unto me,

Starlight and dewdrops are waiting for thee;

Sounds of the rude world heard in the day,

Lull'd by the moonlight have all pass'd a way!

Neema remembered the lines they had read while at college. She flung the emptied bottle and continued:

Beautiful dreamer, queen of my song,

List while I woo thee with soft melody;

Gone are the cares of life's busy throng,—

Beautiful dreamer, awake unto me!

Aparna raised her bottle of Remy Martin and trolled:

Beautiful dreamer, out on the sea

Mermaids are chanting the wild lore lie;

Over the streamlet vapours are borne,

Waiting to fade at the bright coming morn.

They chuckled and serenaded as they turned to go back hand in hand:

Beautiful dreamer, beam on my heart,

E'en as the morn on the streamlet and sea;

Then will all clouds of sorrow depart,—

Beautiful dreamer, awake unto me!

Beautiful dreamer, awake unto me!

---------------------*THE END* ---------------------

ABOUT THE AUTHOR

Nagalakshmi M G., also known as Ashmi is a writer, educator, and counsellor. After having worked as a lecturer in English for over twenty five years in Bangalore, she took voluntary retirement in the year 2001 to pursue her passion for writing. She did her Bachelor of Arts from Kerala University and pursued a Master's degree in English language and Literature at Jnana Bharathi (Bangalore University). Additionally, she has a Degree in M.Phil, and also went on to fulfil her dream of getting a Post Graduate Diploma in Journalism and in 'Proficiency in Counselling' from Bharatiya Vidya Bhawan and The Theological College respectively.

She has published light reads in Femina and The Indian Express. 'A Darling in Your fifties' is her first work of fiction. Although a staunch Bangalorean, she currently lives in Pune with her family.